Melissa

Hathaway House, Book 13

Dale Mayer

MELISSA: HATHAWAY HOUSE, BOOK 13
Beverly Dale Mayer
Valley Publishing Ltd.

Copyright © 2020

This is a work of fiction. Names, characters, places, brands, media, and incidents are either the product of the author's imagination or are used fictitiously. Any resemblance to actual events, locales, or persons, living or dead, is entirely coincidental.

ISBN-13: 978-1-773364-19-3
Print Edition

About This Book

Welcome to Hathaway House. Rehab Center. Safe Haven. Second chance at life and love.

Health-care worker Shane has been at Hathaway House since the beginning. He's watched patient after patient scratch and claw their way to recovery and has watched relationship after relationship blossom into love and marriage. He believes in love. Wants a true love of his own. Yet he wonders now whether anyone is out there for him.

Until Melissa walks into his gym.

Broken and beaten by life and overwhelmed with endless pain was never part of Melissa's long-term plan. But a year after an accident sidelined her navy career, she's still fighting her way back to a normal life—if such a thing exists for the woman she's become. Her transfer to Hathaway House is a lifeline to her oldest friend, but, even with Dani's encouragement, Melissa's journey back to health is long and hard and maybe just a pipe dream. But she'll try again. One more time.

Separately, Shane and Melissa have been battling their own personal demons. When they meet at Hathaway House, the tough physiotherapist vows that his newest client will reach successes unimaginable to her. Together, working through her rehab plan, Shane and Melissa find a special tenderness behind each other's strength.

Sign up to be notified of all Dale's releases here!

https://geni.us/DaleNews

Books in This Series:

Prologue

A T TIMES IN Melissa's life, she'd made rash decisions. Most of them had turned out okay. Sometimes not. Then sometimes she deliberated for so long that the opportunities passed her by.

She stared at the crumpled letter in her lap. Not just crumpled but also tearstained. Her one and only friend had gone to the trouble to track her down, even after years of silence. Then Dani had known Melissa before her parents' death. Afterward she'd moved into Dani's place as a retreat. They'd finished school together. Then Melissa had entered the navy and what she had hoped would be a brand-new life.

And it had been, ... until her accident.

Now she was at a crossroads yet again. And this time, once more, Dani offered a pathway open to Melissa. Back then Dani had pleaded with Melissa to continue staying with her and her father and to not go into service. She'd chosen the navy over her friend back then.

Now Melissa had a chance to choose Dani this time. She had spent the last many years building up a VA rehab center called Hathaway House—originally set up to help her father regain a life after his own injuries had sidelined his military career. With the upstairs part of this center growing quickly to assist human patients, Dani had quickly installed a veterinarian clinic down below. Then that was Dani; she

1

couldn't help herself from trying to save the world, one person, one animal at a time.

Just as Dani had tried to save Melissa back then, she was trying to save Melissa now.

She had refused back then, but now …

Looking around her four-person room, Melissa took in the apparatus attached to her bed, the wheelchair, and the crutches close by. The life she lived here, while recovering from her latest surgery, was filled with hopelessness at the thought of staying here. In reflection, going into the navy had felt like she was running away instead of running to a new future.

Now it felt the same again.

On impulse she picked up her phone and called Dani. When Melissa heard her friend's voice, her throat closed.

"Hello? Hello?"

"Dani," she finally got out.

Silence. Then Dani exploded, "Melissa?"

"Yeah," she said, half in tears, half in laughter.

"Oh my, I'm so glad you called. I'll be even happier if you have filled out that application to come here. Have you?'

"No, I haven't. At least not yet."

"Please do it," Dani pleaded. "We can help you here."

"I don't know if you can," she whispered back. "I'm in pain all the time. The journey itself will be incredibly hard."

"Yes, it could be," Dani said quietly. "But, once here, we have specialists on staff who can help you."

Melissa sniffled back her tears. She wanted to believe her friend. She really did. But hope was a little thin on the ground.

"Please," Dani said into the phone. "Take a leap of faith. Let me help. Last time I pleaded with you to stay. This time

I'm asking you to come. You needed someone back then and walked away. You need someone now. Please don't walk away from me this time."

Melissa took a deep breath and capitulated. "All right. I just hope you know what you're doing."

"I do," Dani said. "Come. You won't regret it."

Chapter 1

M ELISSA DEVEROL OPENED her eyes, hating the hot tears that still rolled down her face. Her gaze frantically searched the room around her to confirm what she already hoped. She was alone. Thank heaven.

The trip to Hathaway House had been brutal. It wasn't supposed to be that way. She was supposed to arrive here in good shape, just the next stop in her healing cycle. But, instead of that, the trip had become something more than just a transfer from one facility to the next. It had become a raging bridge that she struggled to cross.

Even before that was the struggle with her application. It had been denied, then accepted, then denied, then accepted, with the doctors causing the difficulties by determining she wasn't ready for such a step forward. And thinking that she would never make it, she'd finally given up, and then it all came together.

But the transfer itself had been beyond painful. Her most recent surgery left her weak and with more muscle damage than she had even thought was possible, and here she was in agony as she lay on her bed, finally at Hathaway. It should have been a triumph; instead it was just sheer torture. Then what did she expect with hip, knee, foot, and shoulder injuries from getting hit in an intersection. The doctors had done what they could. Now it was up to her body to do the best it could. She could only hope it would be enough.

When she heard a knock on her door, she deliberately closed her eyes, hoping that nobody would come in. But when the door opened, she peered through her damp eyelashes to see a tall blond male step forward.

"Are you okay?" he asked in a warm liquid voice. "I saw you in the hallway when they brought you in. I could see your pain levels. Your team will be here soon, and I'm one of that team," he said. "I'm Shane Roster."

His words came out so smoothly, they almost melted her heart. Actual emotions and genuine concern were in his voice. Which shouldn't surprise her. After all, the two busy nurses she'd dealt with here so far were a nice change.

"I'm the head of the Physiotherapy Department here at Hathaway House."

Her eyes opened fully as she looked up at him. "How did you know I wasn't asleep?"

He gave her the gentlest of smiles and said, "Experience."

She winced. "Are we all such a mess when we arrive?"

"No," he said. "Not at all. But I could see your pain. I could see the stiffness in your spine. I just want you to know that it will get better."

Her eyes widened. "Well, thank you for that," she said, "because I'm not sure it can get much worse."

At that, he shook his head. "It can," he said, his voice firm. "It can get much worse. But we're here to help you get to be the best that you can be."

"Well, first, it'd be nice to stop crying," she said, hating that it always devolved to some female weakness of crying. "I'm not normally so weepy," she explained.

"Tears are just a release," he said, stepping farther into

the room. "They're natural. They're normal, and they're good to help you let go of pain, tension, and stress. You need that release. Don't hold it back. It will just add to your own trauma."

She stared at him, marveling at his words, yet questioning it all.

He smiled and shrugged.

"I thought guys hated women's tears," she said.

"Then they're in the wrong business, if that's the case here," he said, "because tears are a very necessary part of your healing. You need to let them go." He took several steps to the doorway. "I'll come back and talk to you in a little bit, but is there anything I can get you now?"

"A new life?"

"Order received," he said, with a big smile that lit up his whole face. "It just takes a little while to process." And, with that, he stepped out and walked down the hallway.

She lay there, surprised not only at his attitude but in the light way that he spoke about her life. It was different from everything else she'd heard and had experienced up until now. Maybe that was a good thing because surely she didn't want to deal with any more bad events in her life. It had been a pretty rough year already, that distant dream of a normal life always delayed by one more surgery, so that her *normal future* looked a long way off. But now that she was here, maybe she would eventually see her new future.

THE NEXT DAY Shane stopped back in at Melissa's room again. For some reason, watching her arrival and transfer had touched him. He'd immediately read her case file. She was almost heartbroken that she couldn't be who she wanted to be, something he'd seen time and time again in patients of his.

But something about her had struck a chord and had pulled at his heartstrings. The fact that Melissa reminded him a lot of his sister, whom he rarely got to see now, was another big aspect to it, and Melissa had looked so much like she needed a friend last night. Just someone to tell her that she would be okay. He knew everyone here had a different version of what that looked like, and it rarely matched reality. Acceptance was part of the process.

When he walked into her room today, he looked around. She was still tucked into bed, hardly having shifted from the previous night, but her eyes were open, and her gaze was clear. "Good morning," he said, noting a spark in her eyes, which was also good. His spirits lifted.

"Good morning, Shane," she said. "I am feeling better today."

"Are you?" he asked. He motioned at the way she was positioned in bed. "Do you shift at all during the night?"

She slowly shook her head. "No. I try not to."

"Because of the pain?"

She nodded slowly again.

"And yet lying in the same position like that," he said, "causes all kinds of other problems. We have to get you up and moving. And we have to get you so that you can shift in the night without that pain. Are you taking medications for it?"

"Yes," she said, "but a lot of times they don't touch the pain."

"Ah," he said. "That figures. Pain is debilitating and causes stress, which then slows healing."

She shrugged. "It doesn't seem to make any difference though, does it?"

"It can," he said. "We just need to keep working on everything that's going on in your world. I haven't done a full assessment, so I can't really see what that looks like yet."

"At this point in time, I think every doctor must come from a completely different program because they all seem to have varied ideas of what to do."

"And have you liked any of your doctors?"

"I did like one," she said wistfully. "But then he ended up working in a new area, and I couldn't go to him anymore."

"And the next doctor?"

"He had another plan for me and changed my program, changed some of the medication, added two new surgeries, and, next thing I know, I'm still not any better."

Such a note of defeatism was in her tone that he worried about her. "How's the depression?"

Her gaze flipped up to his. "I didn't say I was depressed." An almost defensive note was evident in her tone.

"How could you not be?" he asked, raising his eyebrows. "Your whole world has been this struggle to get back to normality."

"And here everybody tells me *this* is normal," she said on a broken laugh. Inside she wondered at his wording. She was afraid to hope that life here could offer much, but at least Shane was approachable and easy to talk to.

"There is no *normal* anymore," he said. "*Normal* is what you make it. *Normal* is when you stop trying to change your condition. Are you ready to stop trying to change this?"

She looked at him, frowned, then slowly shook her head. "No. That's why I'm here."

"Good answer," he said, his smile bright.

She frowned at him. "Do you think you can help?"

"Absolutely," he said. "I just don't know what, how much, or how long it'll take. Remember? It's a journey."

"And if I'm not up to traveling?" She hated to be negative, but she'd heard so much from so many that she'd more or less lost hope.

"We'll take the journey at your speed," he said, staring intently at her.

She nodded slowly. "You know something? I want to believe you."

"Meaning, you've been let down before, and you've been disappointed by the results of your surgeries, and you haven't found the same optimism that everybody else was trying to cheer you up with?"

"Exactly." She laughed. "It's almost like you've heard this a time or two."

"Much more than a time or two," he said. "And the thing is, one doctor will have one opinion, and another doctor will have another opinion. But individually, it's your body, and what works for you and how a procedure will turn out is something that nobody can tell you with any degree of certainty. And we have to work with what the result is, so we can improve on it."

"And again, it all sounds good," she said. "And I want to believe you, but …"

"Then do," he interrupted quietly. "First things first though, we have to get you to the point that you're not in so much pain."

"I don't even recognize the pain anymore," she said.

"I can see that, and that's part of the problem too," he said, "because then you're not shifting to get away from it anymore. You're just locking yourself down and ignoring the pain receptor messages coming to your brain."

"Yes, but, if I listen to the messages, it hurts," she said. "Remember? I'm trying to get away from the pain."

"I remember," he said cheerfully. "How much of your team did you meet and see last night?" he asked, changing tactics.

She frowned. "I saw a couple people, but I don't necessarily remember who they were."

"That's normal. It's a bit overwhelming when you first get here," he said, "but it will improve."

"You sound … Are you always this positive?" she asked.

"No, not always, but there's nothing wrong with being positive," he said. "It helps get you where you need to go. You should meet the rest of your team today." He sounded confident but stopped, studied her for a long moment, then asked, "How ambulatory are you?"

"I can walk fine," she said with a shrug.

"I wonder what that means to you. And if it means the same thing to me."

She turned toward him. "Sorry?"

He smiled and changed the subject. "Have you had a tour of the place?"

She winced at that. "No. That sounds like too much work."

"Because walking is too much work?"

"I can, though, but would prefer not to. Walking hurts, so I don't do much of it."

He nodded, walked to the side of the bed, pulled out the wheelchair that was in every room, and brought it closer to her. "Let's do a quick tour."

"I don't think that's a good idea," she protested.

He noted her fingers, gripping the sides of the bed until her knuckles turned white. "Is the pain bad right now?"

She took a long, slow, deep breath. "Sometimes."

"Have you eaten?"

She shook her head. "I don't eat much."

"Another reason why your body isn't doing as well as you would like."

"They say I'm supposed to feed it," she said, "but food isn't anything I particularly like. It's like everything in my world has changed. My taste buds are different. Food tastes different."

"That's not uncommon either," he said. "However, we do have good food here, and it's very important that you get up and move around."

"But sitting in a wheelchair isn't *moving around*," she said.

He looked at her, pinned her in place with his gaze, and asked, "You want to walk?"

Her lips thinned. "This isn't a question as to whether I want to leave my room," she protested. "You're saying it's not a choice."

"No, right now, it's not a choice," he said, straightening up, looking at her carefully. "It's all about understanding who you are as a person and how willing you are to do what needs to be done."

"And going for breakfast needs to be done?"

Such a note of disbelief was in her voice that he had to laugh. "You need to see your new home," he said. "You need to take a look at the world that is now *your* world. And, while we're at it, we'll find you some food, yes. And, if you have special dietary needs, then we'll talk to Dennis about it." As he walked over, he didn't give her a chance to argue but flipped back the covers, reached down, gently swung her legs around to the side, and had her sitting on the edge of the bed before she had time to argue.

She stared at him in shock, as her body struggled to stay balanced in place. "You're very good at that."

"I am," he said, with that lethal smile of his.

"Bet the ladies love it," she muttered.

He broke out laughing. "Not exactly my normal bedside style."

"Probably a good thing," she said. "That doesn't always work for everybody. It's a little too masterful."

"There's a time to be masterful, and there's a time not to be," he said. "When somebody's being stubborn, it's time to take charge."

"Gee," she said. "Thanks for that."

"You're welcome," he said, ignoring her grouchiness. "Now, are you ready to get out, or will I just pick you up and put you in the wheelchair?"

"Well, if you put it that way," she said, as she reached out a hand, and he gave her an arm for support, while she slid to her feet and stood. She took a deep breath and straightened.

"So tell me something," he said. "Do you consider yourself standing right now?"

She looked at him and said, "Of course."

He just nodded and said, "Into the wheelchair with you."

She took a few steps to the wheelchair and then sat down carefully to avoid a spike in pain. But, with every movement, she tried to ward off the sudden anguish.

"Interesting," he muttered to himself.

"I don't think *interesting* is quite the right word," she

muttered, feeling more than shaky. Not exactly a strong and in-control movement.

"Oh, it is," he said. "Half of the battle is decoding what the problem is."

"Well, you should have my file," she said. "You'd see lots of problems."

"And I'll get to it," he said. "I took a quick look already but need to delve deeper."

"What? Another doctor who doesn't look or do his homework?"

"I prefer to do my homework in person," he said, ignoring her attitude. "And I'm not a doctor."

She shrugged and said, "Do you think you know more than the doctors?"

At that, he burst out laughing. "Absolutely not. Our educations are extremely different. The doctors do what they do, and then I take over."

"Interesting." But, by then, he already had her rolled out in the hallway. She looked around with interest. "I hadn't expected it to be so big."

"It's very big," he said. "We're up to several hundred beds by now."

"So how come I have your attention if you're the head of PT?"

"Well, we're all assigned to teams for various patients. I had several patients go home, so some of my workload is reduced. Now I have new patients," he said cheerfully. "Of which you are one."

"And it doesn't have anything to do with the fact that I'm friends with Dani?"

He looked at her in surprise. "Are you?"

"Yes," she said. "We went to school together."

"Interesting," he said. "Why didn't you come here earlier then?"

She hesitated and then shrugged. "Maybe because I'm stubborn?"

"I hadn't noticed," he said.

She burst out laughing. "I guess I can be a bit of a grouch," she said. "I'm sorry about that."

"You're not sorry about it. It's a defense mechanism," he said. "It's normal from someone in your situation."

She groaned. "Do you have an answer for everything?"

"Nope," he said. "It's up to you to find the answers, not me." He watched the frown form on her face at that. He knew he took things a little bit differently than a lot of people, but he also needed to shake her up a bit. Just so much negativity was in her world that she had to let some of it go in order to find the progress that she desperately wanted. The question was, did she want it enough to do the work to get there?

Because that was a whole different story.

Chapter 2

A S SHANE PUSHED her forward, Melissa noted how many private rooms were here, how wide and open and spacious the center was. "It doesn't look like a hospital," she said cautiously.

"That's because it isn't a hospital."

"Okay, but it doesn't resemble a VA center either."

"How long were you in one?"

"A few months," she said with a shrug, then winced because that shrug hurt too. "Basically, I feel like somebody took my body and tossed me off a high wall. Just call me Humpty Dumpty."

He chuckled at that. "We've seen a few of those here."

And something about him not being shocked or worried made her relax even further. "Well, it's nice to know that it's not necessarily something you haven't seen before," she said slowly. "But I wouldn't want you to think that, just because you *may* have seen something like me before, I'll be the same as everybody else."

He leaned over and said, "You're not like anybody else. We'll treat you as an individual. Give us a chance."

And, with that, she had to be satisfied.

They approached a huge area, some common area for recreation with a pool table, card game tables, even huge TVs mounted on several walls.

"Well, this is a nice spot," she said. "It's empty though."

"That's because everybody's heading for breakfast."

She laughed. "Well, that in itself would be a good sign, if people cared to get to breakfast on time."

"The food is wonderful here, and, if you especially want something, just tell us."

"Well, I'm really big on eggs," she said. "I love my veggies too."

"You'll get both here," he promised.

"Neither are particularly hard to supply," she said, "but doing them right? Now that's a whole different story."

"Do you cook?"

"I do," she said, "or at least I used to."

"It's not something you have to stop doing, is it?"

"It's not like I've had an opportunity to do any," she said with half a smile. "I'm stuck with things in place. I mean, I haven't had space where I can do a whole lot."

"What other hobbies have you stopped doing?"

"I don't know," she said. "Most anything that requires movement." And then she gave a broken laugh. "I don't mean to sound so whiny about everything," she said. "That's really not who I am. But, when you ask the questions, some of them are hard to answer."

"Do you read?"

"Yep," she said. "I love thrillers."

"Do you do anything with your hands, such as knitting, crocheting, painting, woodwork? Anything like that?"

She shook her head. "No. I haven't done anything like that for a long time. I used to garden."

"Gardening is good," he said. "It's a gentle hobby that reconnects people to their basic needs. You should be able to resume that hobby down the road. We need to work on balancing out your body and strengthening the muscles first."

It made her smile to think she might be able to grow things again—even if only a few herbs and tomatoes. There was nothing like fresh tomatoes from a garden.

By then they had entered another huge room, the cafeteria space, a line of people along the right side opposite masses of tables. The kitchen must be behind the doors on the right side too.

"Well," she said.

Then he leaned forward and said, "You'll have to talk loud up here."

She realized the din of the place was the second effect that really surprised her. "A lot of people are here," she said. And that, in itself, was almost intimidating.

"There are," he said. "You want to go out on the deck and take a look first or get in line?"

She looked at the line and shrugged. "That doesn't look like it'll go anywhere quickly, so let's go out on the deck."

He headed her wheelchair through the tables until they got to an open-air deck with great big sliding glass doors that separated most of the deck, but they were wide open right now. And he said, "You can sit out here in the sun or in the shade."

She was amazed at the space. But then her gaze caught the green hills before her on the other side of the deck. "Can you take me over there?"

He pushed her forward to where she could see over the edge of the railing. When she saw the horses running across the field, she cried out, "Horses!"

"I thought you were Dani's friend?"

"Well, Dani and I were always horse crazy back then,"

Melissa said, shaking her head, "but I had no idea horses were here."

"Did she not tell you about the animals?"

"She did, it's just hard to envision without being here." She tilted her head at him. "Is there much more?"

"There absolutely is more," he said. "A whole vet clinic is downstairs. They work on injured animals and do basic care for all animals, plus they run a lot of fosters through there. We have therapy animals from downstairs that visit the human patients up here, and several dogs, cats, and horses are permanent residents here too. Of course, out there is Lovely, the llama. We have a little filly out there too. Midnight is Dani's horse." He pointed out Midnight, who stood at a fence, leaning over and accepting long grass from somebody in a wheelchair.

"Wow," she whispered. "That's huge."

"Are you an animal lover?"

"Absolutely," she said. "Especially dogs." Then she pointed. "Who's that one?"

"That's Helga," he said with a chuckle. "She's one of the therapy dogs who doesn't know she has only three legs. Couldn't care less either."

"She's huge," she said.

"She's a Newfoundlander, and, as far as she's concerned, her size makes no difference. She thinks you still should be cuddling her twenty-four hours a day."

At that, Melissa chuckled. "Oh, wow," she said. "Dani really created something here, hasn't she?"

"She has, indeed. And now you know why she wanted you to come."

"Yes," she said, "and she knew that I was a big animal lover to boot."

"Good," he said. "The line is going down, so let's go back and get you some food."

"Can I bring it out here?"

"You sure can," he said. "It's all part and parcel of the whole deal."

"Good," she said. "I would like to spend as much time outside as I can."

"Vitamin D is very important," he said. "You need about four hours a day in order to get what you need."

"I thought it was only like twenty minutes," she said jokingly.

"Well, it certainly isn't four hours. I was making sure you were listening to me," he said with a laugh. "But you can get quite a bit of time outdoors. Once we get you into the pool, that will help too."

"And a pool?" she said, twisting gingerly and slowly to look at him a minute. "Is that for us or for the staff?"

"For everyone," he said, nodding. "We'll start some of your physiotherapy there, once we have an idea of where you're at for mobility. You swim?"

"I was navy," she said. "I swim."

"Good," he said. "That makes it a little easier."

"It must be hard to have somebody who doesn't swim."

"On the other hand," he said cheerfully, "it's a great time for them to learn to swim."

"Wouldn't that be nice," she said. "I'm looking forward to the pool. When can I get in there?"

"Not for a while," he said. "We have days of testing."

"That does not appeal," she said in a grumbling voice.

"Maybe not, but it's very necessary."

Just then they pulled up through the crowded cafeteria, and the din was once again overwhelming. "Everybody's so loud."

He bent closer to her ear. "But it's a happy loud," he said. "If you listen to it, you'll hear that it's just people being people."

She tilted her head, as she assessed some of the chatter around her. But he was right. It wasn't upsetting. It wasn't cries. It wasn't anger. It was conversation. It was *Good morning* and *How are you?* and *How was your night?*—that type thing.

And, before she realized it, he had her in a line, and they headed alongside the buffet offerings. He grabbed a tray for her and kept pushing it forward.

She looked at it and said, "I could walk, you know."

"Not right now," he said. As they came up to one of the glass counters, he called out, "Dennis."

A huge man came to the front counter, leaned across the top, and smiled down at her. "Now that's a new face I haven't seen before."

She smiled up at him. "I'm Melissa," she said. "I just got here last night."

"Uh-huh," he said. "So I see they wouldn't let you skip breakfast, huh?"

She shook her head. "No, Shane was pretty much against that."

"We're all against that," he said. "You need your food."

She smiled up at him. "But what if I'm not hungry?"

"We always have something to be hungry for." He quickly explained how the kitchen worked, how the coffee and tea were always here. Food was always here. If she ever woke up hungry, she could raid the self-serve fridge filled with sandwiches, muffins, quiches, things like that. All beside a microwave, if needed. "And," he said, "I have lots of hot fresh food now. What do you prefer for breakfast?"

She raised both eyebrows. "Wow! I haven't been asked that in a long time."

"Well, that was then. This is now," he said, "and food is a big part of your healing. But the right food."

"Oh, I agree with that," she said. "What do you have?"

"I've got eggs, sausages, bacon, omelets, fresh fruit, yogurt, homemade bread, French toast. If that doesn't appeal, tell me what does. Oh, we also have muffins today. What would you like?"

Just then her stomach growled. She stared at him, a bit embarrassed. "I haven't heard that sound in a long time," she said. "Something triggered it nicely."

"Well, if you haven't eaten, and you're not working out today because it's still not a whole first day for you," he said, "let's get you a decent breakfast. Then you will have lots of energy to hold you over, and you won't have to worry about your stomach getting upset from Shane's workouts."

She looked at Shane. "You already have a reputation, huh?"

"Maybe," he said cheerfully, "but we won't worry about that right now." He looked at Dennis and said, "She told me that she loves eggs."

Dennis smiled, looked down at her again, and asked, "So poached, scrambled, fried? Or how about a spinach and bacon omelet?"

"I'd love that," she said. "Are you sure though? That's more work."

He laughed. "I'm very sure. I'll have it up in a few minutes," he said. "Make sure you get the rest of what you want, and I'll bring the omelet to you."

And, with that, Shane moved her a little farther down

the counter. He asked, "You want some yogurt, some berries, muffins? Anything here?"

A whole pile of add-ons went with breakfast. She grabbed a parfait that looked like half the size of the other parfaits. It was full of yogurt, berries, and granola. "I like this," she said, "but I don't want to take so much food that I can't eat it all."

"And that's a good thing," he said, "because we do have to watch that people eat what they take."

"Right," she said. "So maybe not this." But she hesitated.

He put it firmly on her tray and said, "If nothing else, we can take it back to your room with you because you'll be in there dealing with a lot of team members, as they come to interview you all day."

"Right," she said. "So for a coffee break."

"And the cafeteria is always open," he reminded her. "If you're ever hungry, you can always come and get food."

She nodded, and they went to the coffee area. He poured coffee for the two of them, which surprised her because she figured he had something better to do than to sit around and babysit her. But he didn't seem to be in any rush to leave. Quietly she wondered at that.

He pushed her back to the outside deck, knowing she craved the sunshine and the sight of the animals. She sat close to the railing as she worked away on her parfait without even thinking about it.

By the time Dennis arrived with the omelet, she had tucked into that without realizing just how much food she was consuming. But the two men noticed.

Dennis quickly took away the empty parfait glass and smiled at her. "See? Just even being here helps bring up the appetite."

"That's not a bad thing," she said. "I've lost a lot of weight from the surgeries."

"That's not allowed at all," he said. "I'm really good at fattening people up." He gave her a big toothy grin and took off, leaving her.

She laughed. "How do you guys stay skinny at this place?"

"Well, for the staff, we work it off," Shane said, chuckling. "But, for everybody who's here to heal, you must remember. Good food is a major part of healing."

"I get it," she said and looked down at the omelet. "Wow!"

"And, if you don't like something, just tell Dennis. He lives to make everybody eat happily."

She smiled and said, "Maybe it won't be so bad being here after all."

"If you were afraid it would be bad," he asked curiously, "why did you come here?"

"Dani persuaded me," she admitted. "And maybe I was just being stubborn. But I hated to impose." She leaned forward and whispered, "I have one of those free beds."

He leaned back and said, "Good. At least you're smart enough to take what was offered."

She sat back, looked at him, and asked, "Doesn't it bother you?"

"Of course not," he said. "We have multiples of those beds that we rotate all the time. Not everybody has full care or access. The navy should have given you full care, though they didn't, did they?"

"My injuries didn't happen while I was in the navy," she said. "I had finished a tour and had just left when I was hit by a vehicle. So technically, I was no longer on active service—one day after leaving the navy."

"So you were at the VA hospital when she offered you a bed here?"

"I wasn't showing any progress there. At least I didn't think so."

"Good for her for bringing you here then," he said. "And it doesn't matter what bed you may have or whether the VA benefits come through for you or not because it's all about your healing, not about how you got here. You are here, so let's make the most of it."

She smiled, nodded. "You're very much a cheerleader, aren't you?"

"Sometimes," he said. "And then there'll be times when you really don't appreciate the heavy taskmaster version of me."

"How many days before that happens?"

He gazed at her with a serious look. "Probably three."

She winced. "So enjoy my holiday while I have it?"

"Enjoy it," he said, "because then you're on the most difficult and the most rewarding journey of your life. One that, without which, we can't get you back to being normal."

"I thought you said normal doesn't exist?" she asked in a challenging voice.

"You're right," he said. "So let's get you to the new normal, which I have seen time and time again. It'll be very different than what you think is normal."

"Get me to walk and to sleep without pain, and I'll be grateful," she said. "Anything above that is sheer gravy."

He laughed and said, "Sure hope you like gravy with everything then," he said, "because we have a lot of work to do."

SHANE WASN'T KIDDING. He'd seen a lot of patients come with myriad attitudes; some felt that they wouldn't succeed and proved themselves correct. Others were sure they could take over the world, and they aced this program in no time. But reality always set in as soon as the testing was over, and he started to work with them.

In her case, it took an extra couple days because, by the time he had all the information he needed and had tested her, he was not impressed with her lack of mobility anywhere. Every movement seemed to cause her pain. Her whole structure, her skeleton, was off-kilter everywhere.

By the time he sat down and explained it to her, she said, "So what you're trying to say is," her tone brave, "that you can't help me."

He studied her, seeing the broken expression of hopelessness on her features. "No, that's not what I'm saying at all. What I'm saying is, we'll have to start with small movements and small challenges in order to make this work."

She took a slow, deep breath. "So you're not giving up on me?"

He stared at her. "No. I'm not giving up on you." And he could sense a relaxation taking over her, as she slumped in place.

"But do you think you can do something for me?"

"I'm sure I can," he said with calm certainty.

He wasn't sure where all this was coming from, but, somewhere along the line, Melissa had figured out that a lot of people couldn't do anything for her, and either they had abandoned her or she'd walked away herself.

"Let's get something straight," he said. "You're here for

the long haul. Whether you're here an extra month or not, it doesn't make a bit of difference. We'll do what we need to do for your body, not just because you want it to happen. You'll also see a shrink while you're here, and you'll deal with a lot of different emotions. Right now, all I'm telling you is that your program will start slow because an awful lot of misalignment is in your frame and because you have weak muscles where other muscles are doing twice the work. And, of course, they're getting tired and fatigued. It's hurting you."

She stared at him and shrugged. "If that was supposed to make any sense, it doesn't really."

"As long as you're okay to get started at the pace that I'm ready to start you at."

"I don't know anything about it," she said honestly. "And I have to trust in somebody, so I might as well put my trust in you."

"Good choice," Dani said from the door.

Melissa looked up and smiled at her old friend. "You sure you want me here?" she asked. "According to Shane, it'll be a lot of work and take longer."

"That's fine," Dani said instantly. "I told you a long time ago that it's not about the money. It's about the healing."

Melissa frowned at Dani. "People say that a lot, but learning to believe and learning to trust, that's a different story."

"And so you must learn to trust," Dani said firmly. She looked at Shane. "Melissa and I went to school together for several years. Then we lost touch."

"That's because I went into the navy," she said with a smile at Shane, but then she turned to Dani. "And you, I'm not even sure what you did."

"I ended up with a military father who was badly injured, and that's how this place came to be," she said with a wave of her arm, indicating the building.

"How is the Major?"

"He is doing wonderfully," Dani said, with a bright smile. "You'll see him in a few days, I think. He's gone down south to visit a friend of his."

"Wonderful," she said. "I was afraid to ask, in case he wasn't around anymore."

"He's around, and he's doing well," she said. "And he remembers you. So if you think you'll get away from him, you'd be wrong."

"Ah," she said. "So all those questions again?"

"Any questions and all questions. You know him. When he wants to know something, he'll ask, and it won't really matter if you feel like answering or not."

"I never was very good at dodging his questions anyway," she said with an affectionate smile. "But I always knew that he was more about keeping you and me happy than anything."

"Those days were a long time ago, weren't they?" Dani said, her voice soft.

"Indeed, indeed. Now it's all so different." Melissa motioned at the body she had.

"That car accident really did you in, didn't it?"

"Not to mention it was on the base, and it wasn't my fault," she said. "And I was done with my tour. I was one day past active service."

"This shouldn't have been an argument," Dani said crossly. "You're still allowed VA benefits."

"Well, whether there is or not doesn't matter at this

point because I am where I am."

"That's true. And where you are is the best place for you to be," Dani said in a positive no-arguing tone. "Shane is the best guy to deal with too."

"Did you sic him on me?" Melissa teased. "Because he might not appreciate that."

"She seems to think that she's getting special treatment because she's your friend," Shane said. "I told her flat-out that's not how we operate here."

"No, we sure don't. Besides, that would be insulting to the rest of my team. They're all good," Dani said. "And Shane will do everything he can to get you back on your feet."

"Well, I can walk," she said.

"Nope," Shane said. "That's not walking. That's doing a hunchback sidestep."

"It's still vertical and still moving forward."

"It is," he said, "but it's nothing to what you'll be doing hereafter. And, in any case, we'll take a video of you to document your improvement."

"Video?" She stared at him. "That would not be a cool idea."

"No, but it's what we do," he said cheerfully. "You have lots to learn yet."

She shook her head, looked back at Dani, and said, "You sure I shouldn't be working with somebody else?"

"You're exactly where you need to be at this moment in time," Dani said with an assurance that left no for doubt. "Now you have to let go and to let the process happen."

"So says you," she muttered, as Dani walked away. Instead of being upset though, Melissa felt pretty weepy around the edges. Nice, if nothing else, to know that she still had a friend here.

"Were you guys close in school?"

"Very," she said. "I'd had a rough time back then. Dani and I were already friends. So was the Major for that matter."

"Ah, we don't know a whole lot about those early years of the family," he said, "so it's good that you can relate to her that way."

"Dani and I never had a problem relating," she said. "I've been the one who's probably had the most difficulty."

"You want to share?"

She smiled and shrugged. "Maybe not right now."

"Good enough." And he left it at that.

She was surprised that he did. She wasn't upset but a little curious as to how he could walk away from it so easily. "It doesn't bother you that I don't want to share?"

"Oh no," he said. "When you're ready, you'll share."

"It's nothing major," she said. "I just had a loss back then that made it very difficult. I ended up joining the navy, so that I could get away and could have some identity."

"A common story," he said.

She nodded. "In many ways, it is, isn't it?"

"And remember," he said, "you're still different. You're still unique. And nobody'll lump you in with the rest of them."

She chuckled. "Makes me sound like I'm a mess."

"Everybody is a mess when they have to deal with reality checks," he said. "It doesn't mean anything." She just smiled, as he got up and said, "Now I want to take some videos."

"You were serious?"

"Absolutely. I'm serious about the work," he said.

She groaned and said, "Where and when?"

"Down in my corner of this world," he said, smiling. "So come on. Let's go." He waited for her to push her wheelchair to the doorway. He knew that she wondered why he wasn't pushing her wheelchair now, but independence was important here. He watched how she handled the wheels, could see her movement, the stiffness in her shoulder and her side. By the time they got to his big gym, he motioned her to the center of the gym. Then he brought out his cell phone. "Now I want you to get up out of that chair and walk to the wall. Then I want you to slowly lower yourself down, so you're sitting on the floor."

She just glared at him.

"We're recording this, so you can see how different it will be in a few months."

"Sure," she said. "I should move better in a few months."

The last surgery wasn't all that long ago, but still she got up and hobbled her way across to the wall. He could see the relief on her face when she hit it. She turned and slowly slid in an uncontrolled movement down until her butt hit and bounced. She winced at that. "I have less padding on my butt than I thought."

He laughed. "That's all right. Dennis will work on that part."

She chuckled. "Well, that's good news then," she said. "I hadn't realized how lacking in that area I am now."

"It's not about beauty here. It's not about fitness," he said. "It's about health and managing whatever you have to deal with, whatever challenge that is, so you can be the best you can be."

"Yeah, yeah, yeah," she said with a wave of her hand. "I've heard it all before."

And he knew where she had trouble. She had almost heard too much of it and didn't believe it anymore. But he knew that they could add a ton of improvement for her. But it had to be with her active participation; otherwise all this would be for naught. And that wasn't something he was prepared to let happen.

Chapter 3

BY THE TIME Shane had done whatever tests he had to do, Melissa was shaking inside and struggling to hide the tremors. She'd been trying to cover it up for at least twenty minutes, but his sharp eagle eyes had noticed, and either he'd ignored it or he had wanted to push through to get something completed on his side. When he finally stopped, he said to her, "Will you ever tell me?"

She glared at him. "You mean that you've been watching me suffer, waiting for me to speak up?"

"I told you not to let me push you past six on a scale of one to ten for pain or exhaustion," he said. "Remember that?"

She frowned because she did but only vaguely. "That was at least an hour ago," she said with a wave of her hand, a mannerism she started to realize she did almost automatically. "Since then, I feel like a whole lifetime has happened."

He chuckled. "Well, the lifetime is the fact that you let it get this far. Yes, I've been watching and waiting to see if you would say *stop* or tell me that you'd had enough."

"If you tell me that I'm supposed to do more, I'll do more," she said readily. "And I honestly forgot about you telling me not to push it past a certain point because I passed that point. Now I'm exhausted."

He nodded, walked over to where her wheelchair sat,

and brought it to her. "And that's what I need you to learn," he said. "It's up to you to get to know your own body, what it can do, what it can't do, to what point it needs to stop, to what point you need to stop so you don't hurt yourself more."

"I didn't think about it," she said, groaning as she sank into the wheelchair. But now her body visibly shook.

He gave a muttered exclamation and said, "Come on. Let's get you back to your bed."

"I feel really rough right now," she whispered.

"And what would make you feel better?"

She shook her head. "If I was at home, I'd have a hot bath. But there's no bathtub in my room."

"No, everything's equipped with sit-in showers," he said. "But I have a hot tub, if you think that would help."

She thought about it a few moments and then said, "I won't make it there," she said. "I'll just go to bed." She couldn't see his face but could hear that he didn't like her answer.

At her doorway, he said, "Quickly get changed, and I'll take you down to the hot tub."

She looked up at him and knew that her face was almost white from the day's efforts. "I don't have the strength," she whispered.

He frowned and stared at her. "I don't want to leave you like this because, when you sank, you sank really far and deep."

"I didn't mean to," she said. She slowly pushed herself to the bed. "I'll be fine. I just need to recuperate." As she struggled to stand from the wheelchair, she started to slip because she hadn't put the brakes on.

Immediately he was there. He lifted her in a smooth

movement, pulled the blankets back, and gently laid her down on the mattress. "I'm coming back with a green shake for you. It's full of vitamins and nutrients."

She looked up at him in horror. "You mean those nasty slimy things that look like they're good for you but taste like dirt?"

He burst out laughing at that. "Yes," he said. "But you're obviously more depleted in other areas too. Have they run a bunch of blood tests on you?"

"They did one," she said, "but I haven't seen any results."

"Well, you're obviously extremely deficient, lacking in strength. We'll have to build that up slowly."

"You mean, slower than today?"

"That was only testing," he let her know.

She wasn't sure how she managed to keep joking, but she was more concerned about him feeling terrible because it's obvious he did. She'd hit this wall many times before. "I've been here before," she said. "I'll just lie here and rest, probably sleep for a bit. Then I'll be much better."

He tucked her up with the blanket, and she snuggled in, trying to find that same spot that allowed the pain to slip away. As soon as she found it, the shaking and tremors eased a bit. "If you could pull that blanket up to my chin, I'll just lie here for a bit."

He did as she asked; then he quickly backed away.

She'd almost say he was running, but, if he was, it wasn't away from her. It was toward something; she just wasn't too sure what. As she lay here, feeling her aches and pain easing, she had to wonder if she would ever find a point in time where she could be on her own again.

She hadn't expected to hit the wall so fast, but some

movements that he'd asked of her, that she'd asked of her body, were some which she hadn't done in such a long time. She wasn't sure if it was shock or serious emotional fatigue or physical exhaustion, but she was done for. She was still trying to relax and to calm down a little bit more, when she figured he'd left at least fifteen minutes ago.

It might be safe to take a few deep breaths.

Cautiously she took a little bit deeper of a breath, well aware that her ribs could seize up if she did that too fast. And that was the worst feeling of all, having a steel rib cage that wouldn't move and made her feel desperate for oxygen. But cramps always happened. Muscle knots that crept through the tendons and the muscles around her ribs and stopped them from expanding. She took another slow breath, a little bit deeper, then another one, feeling the oxygen seep in through her lungs.

Realizing that she wouldn't have a cramp, she took yet another, slightly deeper breath, and relaxed into her bedding. "At least it's not too bad now."

"It was bad enough," she heard from the doorway.

She looked up to see Shane standing there. She did her best not to cringe, but she knew he'd seen it.

He held out the green drink to her, tilting the straw so she didn't have to move, and said, "Take a good sip."

She took a small sip, not a good one, giving him a sideways glance.

He smiled at her and said, "All of it," as if she were a two-year-old.

She found her voice and said, "I can't drink it all so fast."

"Maybe not," he said, "but you haven't had more than a tiny bit. Finish what you have left."

She groaned and took a decent amount, tasted it, then wrinkled up her face.

"Apple juice, some mangoes blended in, and a whole pile of supplementation," he said. "Your body is extremely depleted in vitamins and minerals. We'll start feeding it properly in order to build up some energy."

"Feeding me *properly*, so says you," she said. "I'm totally okay to eat food, you know?"

"Good," he said. "But the amount of vegetables that you would need to eat to get the same amount as this supplementation has? You couldn't possibly eat that much."

She frowned. "I could try."

"Nope. This just became part of your normal everyday habit."

"And if I don't want it?"

He stopped, looked at her, and said, "I thought you wanted to get better."

"That's cheating," she said.

"Whatever works," he said with a big smile.

She shook her head, pulled one arm out from under the bedding, and grabbed the glass from him. "Will they all taste like this?"

"No, they'll be different variations on the basics," he said. "The bottom line is, it's one of the easiest ways to get this much nutritional value down you."

"Fine," she said. "It still doesn't taste very good."

"You'll get used to it," he said. "It's really not an option for you."

"Right," she said, heeding his warning. She understood what he was saying. It was just that she'd never been a shake person, never took vitamins or any other supplementation, and found it hard to do so at this stage too.

He looked at her, laughed, and said, "It really will get better."

"Uh-huh," she said, not believing him in the least. He was the guy who would tell her what she needed to hear. And whether it was the truth or not, well, the jury was out on that. She didn't know him well enough. But she knew she was caught in a system here to help support her, and, if she didn't let them do that, she wouldn't be giving it a full test, and then how would she know if it was any good or not?

He stepped back and said, "Make sure it's all gone. I'll be back in a few minutes."

As soon as he was gone, she set the glass down and sank into the bed. Did he mean that she had to have it all drunk by the time he came back? Because that might be a bit much for her stomach. She was also drinking what water she needed to drink, but this was a lot of liquid. And a lot of liquid meant she would have to go to the bathroom a whole lot faster than she really wanted to. But still, if he was coming back, she didn't want to be caught without it gone. She picked it up again and valiantly took a big drink. It didn't seem to be quite so bad this time. She took another big drink and then another one.

By the time he came back, she had it over half gone. He looked at it and nodded. "See? It's not that bad."

"It's not that good either," she said, trying for some spirit. She didn't want him to think she was a complete pushover.

"It doesn't matter," he said. "It will make a huge difference in your body."

"Good." She took another big drink and set it down.

He looked at it and said, "Can you get the last bit down?"

"You're sending me to the bathroom. You know that, right?"

He grinned. "What goes in must come out."

"So it makes sense to stop now," she argued.

He just chuckled and held out the glass for her. She groaned and sucked back the last of it. When she finally set it down, he looked at it and nodded. "Perfect. We'll see how your stomach handles it tomorrow." He turned and walked out with the empty glass.

"Wait. When do I work with you again?"

"Tomorrow," he said, looking back at her. "Remember? You have your schedule in your tablet."

"Oh. I thought maybe you'd push it off because of today."

"No," he said cheerfully. "No time to push off anything. We went a little too far, too fast today, so we'll adjust it tomorrow."

"And does that make it easier?"

"Not likely," he said, his lips tilting up at the corners. "When you think about it, it just means we'll stop where we should have stopped today."

"Sounds easier."

"Well, it may seem easier maybe, but I doubt it." And, with that, he gave her a finger wave and left.

She sagged back, wondering how her life had changed. But she didn't have much time to contemplate it. When she looked up, Dani walked toward her from the hallway.

"How are you settling in?" she asked, her tone a little worried.

"I'm doing okay," she said. "It's a lot to get used to."

"It is, but we're not that different from any other system."

"No," she said. "You are different, but I had adjusted to the other center, so I'll adjust to this one too."

"It's all about making sure you get what you need," she said comfortably. She smiled. "It looks like Shane gave you one of his green juices. Did he?"

"What? They're infamous?"

At that, Dani burst out laughing. "Maybe," she said, "but they're very effective."

"And how did you know?" she asked.

Dani reached out and touched the corner of her mouth. "Because your lips are still covered in it."

She groaned. "He didn't say anything to me about that."

"Nope, he wouldn't," she said. "Not sure he would even have noticed."

She rolled her eyes at that. "How is that even possible?"

"Well, for one, he's a guy," Dani said with a smirk.

"True enough." She paused. "I can't believe you pulled together this center," she said, studying her friend. "And you look so happy."

Dani gave her a bright smile. "Well, I found a purpose in life. I found a passion to follow, and my heart's full of love for somebody who loves me back," she said. "It's hard to be upset with any of that."

"No, I hear you there," she said. "You told me a little bit about Aaron but not a whole lot."

"Well, there's just so much that, once I get started," she said, "I have a tendency to not know when to stop."

"Nothing wrong with that."

Dani looked at her. "What about you? Boyfriends?"

"No," she said, frowning, shaking her head. "After this? Are you kidding? I'm trying to reconcile myself to being alone for the rest of my life."

Dani's eyes twinkled. "Well, this place has gotten a reputation," she said, "for a ton of matchmaking going on here, although not necessarily on purpose."

"What do you mean by matchmaking? With the staff?"

Dani studied her for a long moment. "You know you won't stay like this forever, right?"

Melissa shifted uncomfortably in the bed. "Sure seems like it."

"I know," Dani said. "But it honestly won't be forever. You won't stay this way. And a time will come when you think that maybe something else could be out there for you, and I'm here to tell you that lots of patients here found love again, even after thinking that they were too broken and were only half of what they used to be for anybody to care."

"I haven't seen any response that was terribly positive from any of the men I've met."

"And I don't think that's necessarily quite true," Dani said, her tone a little cautious. "I think we often view everybody from our own lens. So, if we see ourselves as broken, we think other people will see the same thing. But it's not true. Everybody sees people from a different perspective, and you have to be open to seeing what they see too."

"Wow. That's pretty Zen words coming from you," she said. "I hadn't realized you became such a guru in this stuff."

"I'm so not," Dani said. "But one of the things I have learned is that our perception often is tainted by our experience, and we need to open up to see that a lot more is to life than just our negativity and our problems and the challenges that we face."

"Maybe," Melissa said. "I'm just not there yet."

"And that's why I'm here to tell you that you will get there," Dani said with the softest of smiles. "And, by the way, I'm really happy that you're here. It's great to catch up with you." With that, Dani headed back to her office, leaving Melissa alone with her thoughts.

"HERE, DENNIS," SHANE said, holding out the empty glass. "We got it down her at least."

"Was there much of a fight?"

Shane chuckled. "Well, a bit of a fight," he said. "Seems to be almost a standard response, regardless of how good it is for them."

"I can understand that," Dennis said. "We've all become big proponents of these shakes. Yet it took time to get the doubters on board."

"But, if they know it's good for them," Shane argued, "you'd think they would step up a little more."

"Some people will accept it blindly. Other people have been lied to or given such optimistic responses to everything they do that they no longer believe what they're doing."

"I think, in Melissa's case, she's been given optimistic outcomes that haven't manifested. So she's more of the belief that it's not so much that we're lying but that we're not based on reality for our outcomes," Shane said.

"And we've seen that before too," Dennis said, grinning broadly. He took the glass from Shane and said, "I'll take it to the kitchen and get it into the dishwasher. What about you? Do you need anything? I think you missed a meal or two today."

"We seem to get busier and busier every day."

"Which is also why you need to stop and look after yourself," Dennis scolded. "You can't be a mother hen to everybody."

"And yet," Shane said, "the longer I'm here, it seems to be the more I do."

"Because you have yet to come up with your own girlfriend."

"I work so much it's almost impossible to even imagine it happening at all."

"Well, I'm pretty sure that'll change over time," Dennis said.

Shane looked at him and asked, "What about you? You're always behind that counter. You haven't got a partner either."

Dennis nodded. "It's something I've been considering, wondering what to do about it," he said. "But, like you said, it's not an easy answer when we work so much. The trouble is, I love my work, so it's not something I want to stop doing."

"Nope. I'm in the same boat, and we're needed here," Shane said quietly. "Both of us. We each have a unique perspective to offer everybody who comes through these doors. And I think it's important that they see that."

"How can I disagree with you there?" he said. "It's amazing just how much people have suffered throughout the years, and all they really needed was a new outlook on life."

"And that's not easy to get," Shane said. He walked over to the coffee area and asked, "How old is the coffee?"

"Let's put on a fresh pot," Dennis said, doing just that, as Shane looked down at the food.

"The last thing I need is more carbs."

"I've got some stir-fry happening in the back. If you want some, we've got a couple staff members who didn't get lunch either."

"I could have a bit of that," he said. "Not too much though."

Dennis disappeared while Shane waited for the coffee to brew, then poured himself a cup of coffee and wandered about the almost empty cafeteria. It was a popular place for meetings, and a lot of the patients would hang out here with their friends. But, at the moment, it was relatively quiet. And he appreciated a lot of the time when the quiet was something he craved, and a lot of the time it was something hard to get a hold of because just so much activity was going on, sometimes even live music.

Lance was setting up more and more concerts, and it was a joy to hear, yet, at the same time, silence was golden. And right now, for whatever reason, maybe because of Melissa, that's how Shane felt. It was nice to see her coming along, but she'd scared him today too, to see that much stubbornness, that much blind obedience, and yet complete lack of regard for her own health and safety.

She had a lot to learn. He knew that he could help her with a lot, but she had to be open and accepting of it. And that was always where a lot of the hurdles were with patients like her. They had to get over that initial stumble and get to the point where they could accept the help and be grateful to get that because then they got thirsty for more, and that was the point in time where it didn't matter what he did. They just wanted more and more and more of their progress; they thirsted for more. They hungered after it and would do almost anything at that point to get better.

He needed her to get there. He knew she was in a tremendous amount of pain, to the point that her mind was almost dulled, and she just accepted what people said and did what she was told, but she didn't really think about it.

And that was worrisome too because he had to get her pain levels down where she took notice of what was going on around her, so that she could fully engage in what she was doing.

His mind wandered on as Dennis said, "Here you go."

Shane turned to see Dennis holding out a plate of beef and veggie stir-fry. He smiled and said, "That looks delicious."

"Remember? You've got to look after yourself too."

Dennis had the advantage, as he could see from his perspective what Shane could not see of himself.

"You have as much hard-headedness as anybody in this place, and you work harder than anybody I know to make sure your patients are doing the best they can," Dennis said. "Don't let yourself fail because of it."

Shane flashed him a smile. "Same to you, buddy. Same to you." He picked up his plate, coffee, and cutlery, then headed to the deck. If he had the time, he would take his meals down to the animals, but lately it seemed like there was never time. They had more and more patients, so many people in need that sometimes he wondered if it was even possible to help them all.

But, when he focused on helping the ones he had been assigned, people in his little corner, then he was doing his best for them. Just not enough time to help everybody. His gaze landed on the horses. Midnight nestled against the little filly. Shane smiled at that because everybody was happy to be with other people on their own terms.

Sometimes they were thrown together, where they had to make the best of a situation. And he knew that Melissa was there. He wasn't exactly sure if she'd chosen to come or whether she'd been convinced to come or whether she figured, *Why not?* Nothing else would do any good. She was a fascinating person, dark, quiet, and she'd obviously been through enough trauma in her life that she had come out on the other side with a lack of trust and a lack of faith.

He understood, but it was just as important for her to rebuild that broken spirit as it was for her to rebuild that broken body. But somehow he had to convince her of that, and he couldn't do it fast. He muttered about that as he ate his lunch. It was, as usual, delicious.

Dani walked outside and sat down in the chair beside him.

Shane looked at her, smiled, and said, "I almost never see you out of your office," he teased.

"And we don't often see you separated from your clients either," she said in the same tone. "Tough day?"

"Just another busy one in the middle of multiple very long and busy days," he said. "You?"

"I've got no arguments," she said. "Life's pretty decent."

He looked at her and smiled. "Don't get me wrong. Life's very decent," he said. "It's just, sometimes, every once in a while, you hit a low spot."

"Just remember who your friends are," Dani said firmly, "because, in a place like this, people don't stay alone long. Not unless they choose it."

Chapter 4

EARLY IN THE morning Melissa woke up. She wasn't even sure why she was awake. She'd been here several days now, and so far had slept late every day. But this morning, guessing by the light outside, she figured it was somewhere near five-thirty, maybe six o'clock. She lay quietly in bed, knowing that she would have to move soon because of a full bladder but not really wanting to deal with the pain of walking there.

Shane had been pretty solid in believing that they could deal and work with that pain, but, so far, they hadn't really done anything after the testing. In fact, the testing had set her back. They hadn't made very much progress since.

He kept saying she wasn't ready; she wasn't ready. She knew she was ready, she just didn't know what it was that he was looking for as a marker to say that she was ready. And she hated feeling like she had to come up with the right answer. It was like being in school, where, on exams, it wasn't so much about knowing the right answer but you had to give the answer the teacher was looking for in order to get full marks. And that was how she started to feel with Shane. And she hated it. Surely that wouldn't go over well here, when everybody was so emotionally delicate.

Even at that she winced. *"Emotionally delicate?"* she whispered. Who would have thought she'd use a phrase like that for herself. But she had spent her lifetime trying to be tough, trying to be one of the guys, part of the group, and honestly, she had finally made a place for herself. But it hadn't been a comfortable fit. She'd made it work in the end, but it hadn't been where her heart was. But then, joining the navy had been a way to escape her ugly life. Plus she'd seen it as a way to belong, a way to have something of a life for herself.

Instead she'd just ended up feeling more isolated. Maybe she'd retreated into a state she knew well. She'd been isolated all her life in so many ways. It was not that she was difficult by any means, but ...

She stopped thinking about it. Yet her mind continued. She was reserved, a little harder to get to know, and that had caused her trouble. A lot of people said that she was cold, introverted, even though that wasn't true. She was just not somebody who spoke openly about her feelings or about the hardships that she'd gone through.

It seemed like everybody in the world had hardships, and that made her feel like hers were relegated to the *so what* category. Although many hadn't seemed to go through what she had gone through, yet to even think like that sounded like she was making excuses. Like she was coming up with a reason to justify her feelings, whereas what she really needed to do was just accept that they existed and stop trying to justify them. She'd heard that advice time and time again from various people, but it wasn't the easiest thing for her to let go.

That was part of the reason she wasn't looking forward to seeing a shrink here. That would mean dealing with a whole pile of history that she wasn't prepared for.

Just around that time, her bladder insisted on being

emptied. Taking a deep breath, she slowly sat up. Then she gingerly swung her legs to the floor. It would take a minute to get some blood circulating through the rest of her as it was, and getting off the bed tended to feel more like a jump instead of just a step. But she made it, finally, in an awkward slide. Standing on her feet, she limped her way to the bathroom.

By the time she was done, she craved a shower. It was early, so she shouldn't have any conflicting issues with that. Inside the shower stall she scrubbed herself from head to toe, loving the feel of the hot water running over her sore shoulders and neck.

As she stood under the water, she slowly did some stretches that Shane had shown her to loosen some of her muscles. They were surprisingly effective. By the time she was done, dried off, and dressed for the day, she had her shoulder-length hair pulled into a hair clip at the back of her head.

She made her way again to the bed and checked her cell phone for the time. It was just seven-thirty. Maybe too early for breakfast but not too early for coffee. She studied the wheelchair and realized that, as much as she didn't want to use the wheelchair, walking down there and back again would wear her out before her day had even begun. It would have to be the wheelchair, whether she liked it or not. She got in and slowly pushed herself out to the hallway and down to the cafeteria. With any luck it might be empty.

As she wheeled through the double doors, she saw that it wasn't empty, but it was definitely calmer and quieter then normal. No food was out on the buffet, so she headed to where the coffee was set up. The man who she had come to recognize as the head of the kitchen area, even if he wasn't the chef, Dennis, stood there putting on fresh coffee. At the sound of her wheels approaching, he turned, looked at her, and a big smile crossed his face.

"Now that's a good sign," he said.

She looked up at him in surprise. "What is?"

"To see you here. Pretty and bright and early."

"And here I thought it was a sign I had a bad night," she said drily.

He laughed. "That too," he said. "But you're up and active, and that's worth a lot."

She wondered at his eternal optimism but was ready to let it go because he seemed so happy. And honestly, that was contagious. "I am hungry."

"Coffee first," he said. "Muffins, yogurt, granola, all kinds of easy breakfast stuff, like fruit balls, are on the sideboard," he said. "And we'll have hot food out any minute now."

"That early?"

"We're running a little behind this morning," he said, "but not to worry. By the time you get your coffee to a table, I'll have the pans out." On that note, he headed behind the kitchen counter and disappeared through the double doors into the back.

She chose a table out in the sun and put her cutlery and coffee down, then turned to go back in inside. And, sure enough, as soon as she was in the line, now two people stood in front of her. Then Dennis came out with a trolley full of trays. She smiled as the covers came off and the trays were put down. Large spoons were put in each, in a very efficient manner, and, all of a sudden, people were serving themselves. They knew how the system worked here. She waited until it was her turn. When she got up to the front, Dennis was there, waiting for her.

"If nothing appeals," he said, "or if you fancy anything else, just let me know."

She shook her head. "This is all good," she said, and she served herself a decent portion, without getting too much. She wanted to make sure that she didn't waste any food, and yet, at the same time, she could feel the hunger gnawing at her belly.

With a full tray on her lap, she slowly wheeled out to where she'd placed her coffee and cutlery. She was careful not to spill anything, but it was dicey. She wasn't even sure how people carried as much as they did. She had never had that skill or coordination to do something so economical when moving about, but they all seemed to handle it quite well.

Crash.

She twisted slowly to see one of the guys standing there with crutches, a tray, and a lost look on his face, as he stared down at what had been one of the yogurt parfaits, which was now smashed on the floor.

"See? I told you, Dennis," he said.

"And I told you that you won't be the first and you won't be the last," Dennis said. Coming around with a mop and bucket, he quickly cleaned up the splattered food, handed the guy another parfait, and said, "Try it with this one."

He looked at him and frowned. "It's obvious I can't do it."

"You *didn't* do it," Dennis corrected. "That doesn't mean you *can't* do it. This time, instead of worrying about where your feet are going, keep your eye on the tray."

And, with that, she held her breath and watched as he

carefully carried the tray and another plate ever-so-slowly. It was a small tray, sure, but he carried it in one hand as he moved with one crutch forward.

"Wow," she said to herself. "I would have been too embarrassed to try again."

And yet not only had he tried but he'd succeeded. He sat down with a huge grin of triumph.

Dennis cheered, adding, "See? Not so hard after all. It's all about coordination."

"And who's got coordination around this place?" Melissa muttered under her breath.

As if Dennis had heard her, he smiled and said, "You'll get there."

She wasn't so sure about that, but she nodded, not ready to start an argument, when all she could see was the food in front of her. She quickly tucked in, enjoying every bite. By the time she was done, Dennis came around with a coffeepot and refilled her cup. "Haven't you got anything better to do?" she asked.

"Sure I do," he said. "Lots of people here need a cup of coffee, but you're one of them too."

"I don't need looking after."

He stopped, gazed at her, smiled a gentle smile, and said, "I'm not so sure about that. It might be that you need more looking after than most." And, on that strange note, he turned and walked away again.

She stared after him, wondering what he meant, when a tray landed on the table beside her, and somebody asked, "Mind if I join you?"

Not that she had a chance to say yes or no because it was Shane, and, as he sat down, she looked at all the food in front of him and whistled. "Wow! How often do you work out to get away with that amount of food?"

"Not enough," he said, laughing. "But Dennis is very good at what he does."

"Does he cook this?"

"No," Shane said, "not at all. Ilse is the head chef, the manager, the all-round kitchen helper. You'll meet her eventually, and a good four or five guys and gals are in the kitchen with her most days as well. But Dennis runs the outside of the kitchen. He always makes sure there's food for us all."

"He does seem to care," she admitted.

"And then some."

SHANE HAD SEEN Melissa sitting there when he arrived in the big room for breakfast. As he loaded his plate, Dennis had a big smile for him, as usual. Shane motioned toward where Melissa sat. "Has she been here long?"

Dennis nodded. "Had a bad night," he said. "She was here really early."

"Maybe I'll see how she is." He picked up his tray and headed to where Melissa sat, asking if he could join her. He didn't really give her a chance to say no. He wasn't sure if she would give him the answer he wanted. It was always easier to take the choice away from somebody. He sat down, studying her. He could see the bags under her eyes and the stiffness in her body, but she seemed to be sitting better. "How was your night?"

She gave an irritable shrug. "It was okay," she said, "but it wasn't great. Most nights aren't great anymore."

"You look stiff."

"You think?" she said, then she shook her head. "Sorry. I'm not trying to be grumpy, but, like I said, I didn't get a whole lot of sleep. I was in here early. I wasn't sure what time I was allowed to come in but decided the lure of coffee was worth the trip."

"If the doors are open," he said cheerfully, "you're allowed in."

"Good," she said. "I don't know. I guess I'm just waiting for something to happen, waiting for some improvement."

He smiled. "I hear that a lot," he said.

She looked past his shoulder, a frown on her face.

He didn't turn around, knowing that she could be looking at any number of things. "Something wrong?" He forked a sausage and took a big bite.

She shook her head, but her gaze was locked behind him. "An animal?" She looked at him, looked back, and then nodded. "A man is carrying something, but I don't know what it is. It's so big though."

"Is it huge, fluffy, with long ears?"

She stared at him and asked, "Have you seen it before?" She pushed back from the table and leaned around him so she could get a better view.

Shane turned, saw Stan with Hoppers, and called out, "Hey, Stan."

Stan took one look and headed toward him.

"Who's Stan?"

He looked at her in surprise. "Did you get a tour of downstairs?"

She shook her head. "No, I haven't been downstairs yet."

"Well, that's something we need to change," he said with a bright smile.

Stan walked over and looked at Melissa. "What's this, a new arrival?"

She smiled up at him and said, "Yes. I've only been here a couple days."

"Well, I haven't seen you downstairs in my corner," he said. "Do you mind if I sit?"

Shane watched as her gaze was locked on the rabbit in his arms. Of course it was big enough to be five rabbits, but she said, "Please join us."

Shane didn't care, even though he was still eating, and some people would be offended, but he was fine with it. Besides, he was almost done. He looked over at Melissa and grinned. "You're staring with absolute fascination at the rabbit. Melissa, this is Stan. He's the vet from the center downstairs. And this is Hoppers," he said, "one of the rabbits he's working on, supposedly to be a therapy animal, I think."

"Well, we could have picked a lighter-weight one," Stan said chuckling, "but everybody has such an interesting reaction when they see him."

Melissa's gaze flew up to look at Stan, then back down again. "My goodness," she whispered, "he's beautiful."

"He is, indeed."

"But why is he here with you?"

"Well, he needs some extra care. He's missing a leg," he said. "He had an injury that we were working on, but then we had to amputate the leg because it just wouldn't heal like it needed to. We've got a big pen for him downstairs, but I do like to bring him up and around to see people. It's good for him to have the interaction, and it's good for the people to have the interaction."

She reached out a hand, then hesitated. "May I?"

Stan smiled. "Absolutely. Hoppers loves people."

She reached out a hand to let Hoppers sniff. His head lifted, and his nose went crazy. She reached out to gently stroke one of his long ears. "He's so silky," she whispered.

"He is, indeed. He's also a big baby," Stan said with a chuckle. "But the baby I can handle."

"You're lucky you work with animals so much."

"Well, it's the field I went into," he said with a smile. "We all have reasons for doing what we do. We just don't always understand what it is until later."

She frowned at his words.

He stood and said, "I'll take Hoppers around to visit a few other people. Then I'll take him back down and let him out into his pen." And, with that, he walked away, carrying Hoppers in his arms.

"It's fascinating," she said, turning to face Shane. "Dani told me that she had animals here, but I thought we were talking about horses, like Midnight."

"Midnight and a llama called Lovely and all kinds of other critters," he said quietly. "Because it's not just a place for people to recover, it's a place for animals to recover too."

"But how could anyone give Hoppers away?" she asked, still watching Hoppers say hi to other patients.

"Often they don't. A lot of the animals stay here permanently. And that's something that Dani plays a big role in. Her charitable contributions go a long way to keeping these animals safe."

"The things you don't really know about a person," she said. "I had no idea that Dani had created something so special."

"You probably haven't kept too close an eye on her in the last few years, have you?"

She shook her head. "No, I guess not. But I hadn't realized that I'd gotten quite so far away from what was going on in her life. I mean, I knew about this place, but I didn't really *know*—if you understand what I mean," she said. "This is stunning. To think that she's done all this makes me wonder what I did with my life."

"Ah," Shane said. "No heading down that pathway. You went into service, and we all appreciate that."

She looked up, smiled, and said, "And yet now I don't really feel like I have done anything."

"That's because you've come from one world to the next. What did you do in the navy?"

"Communications officer," she said quietly. "I did it because I fell into it, and I was good at it. I'm not sure it's something I would want to continue to do."

"Good enough," he said. "Nobody said that you had to do the same thing all the time. Variety is often the spice of life. And sometimes, when we make a change, like you've done right now, some people cling to the old world because it's familiar. For many others, they just want something completely different from what they used to do. Sometimes they don't have a choice. Sometimes what they did is something they can no longer do, and they're looking at a complete career change."

She nodded. "Well, I certainly could do some of what I was doing back then," she said, "but I'm not sure it's what I would want to do."

"Any idea what you would want to do?"

She smiled and shook her head. "No, I don't think so. At this point in time, just getting healthy and back on my feet seems like a big-enough issue."

"Not an issue," he said, "but definitely something you have to commit to."

"I guess that's what I meant," she said. "It's a big-enough commitment right now that it's hard for me to look past it."

"Nobody said you had to," he said comfortably.

She smiled at him. "Are you always this amiable?"

His eyebrows shot up. "Most of the time, yes," he said. He studied her features, wondering what was his attraction to Melissa because he had a lot of patients around here. He could certainly have sat with anybody, but just something about being with Melissa intrigued him. Maybe it was the absolute brokenness of her body that attracted him. And, man, that said, he needed to rethink where he was mentally. But it wasn't that her body was so broken as much as it was the struggle with her spirit. She was trying to get her body back together again and functioning the way it needed to. Her spirit was there; it was just hiding, and he wanted it to come out of hiding and do so much better than what it was right now. "Are you ready for today?"

"Is today something I need to be ready for?" she asked.

He smiled and said, "Yes, absolutely."

"Okay," she said. "Well then, I guess the answer is no, I'm not ready."

"Too bad," he said cheerfully, as he stood up. He checked his watch. "I'll see you in fifteen minutes in the exercise room." He turned and walked away. He lifted a hand to Dennis and called out, "See you at lunchtime."

"I'll be here," he said with a big chuckle.

And that was the thing that Shane loved about this place—the people in it, the consistency of the work they did, and the growth and joy that they could bring to the patients' faces. It didn't come easy, and often it took a long time to happen, but, when it did, it was worth every moment he put into it.

Chapter 5

MELISSA WAS A little trepidatious as she sat in her wheelchair at the entrance to the gym. Shane was there, marking something down on a tablet. He had the computer set up, charts off to the side, but the equipment around the room was intimidating. She'd seen it all before and knew the agony of using most of it.

He didn't look up but said, "I don't bite. Come on in. Shut the door behind you too, please."

That seemed even more ominous. She closed the door and slowly wheeled toward him. "Did you create a plan for me?" she asked with a light voice.

"Yep," he said. "At least one to start with."

"Meaning?"

"Meaning, we'll have to adapt it as we go," he said, "as we always do."

"Why?"

"Because some exercises could have different results. Don't worry," he said. "We won't go too far, too fast. We'll do our best to minimize the pain."

"Is that even possible?" she asked.

"To minimize, yes. To stop all of it, no, not in PT at least," he said, "because the whole idea is to force these muscles to work again. They've been sleeping, and they need to wake up, step up, and do the job. But we don't want to shock them or force them. We want to coax them into doing it."

She shook her head. "Sounds like a lot of pain to me."

He looked up, smiled at her, and nodded. "It won't be pain-free, that's for sure. But one of the first things I want to work on is the fact that you're in so much pain now."

"Well, that's not something you can fix easily."

"No, it isn't, but it is something we work at on a steady basis."

She waited.

"We'll start on the floor," he said. "So down on the mat on your back, please."

She groaned but managed to get down there. It was almost halfway a collapse. When she made it to the mat in the position he'd asked for, she closed her eyes and said, "Okay. Let's do this."

Two hours later she lay here, shuddering on the floor. He sat beside her and said, "You're still not willing to let me know when the pain is too strong, are you?"

"I'm not sure if it's a case of not being willing," she whispered, "as much as it's potentially something I don't recognize."

"And that's a good answer," he said. "I think you've been disassociated from your body for so long because of the pain, because of the brokenness, that you haven't been in tune to what it needs, what its own needs are."

"Maybe," she said. "But, when you have many health problems, it's a lot easier to ignore it all than to figure out which parts are working and which parts aren't."

"Understood," he said, "and that's why I'm here. We'll get it figured out." He straightened. "That's enough for now."

"Good," she said. "I couldn't do any more."

"I'm glad to hear that."

She looked at him in surprise. "Why is that?"

"Not that you're done," he said, "but that you're finally realizing that you can tell me that you're done."

"Well," she said with half a smile, "I don't have a great record with relationships. Including therapists."

"In what way?" he asked, standing with his hands on his hips.

She shook her head. "It's nothing to do with you."

"It has everything to do with me," he said. "At any point in time, where something's blocking your healing, it matters to me."

"Yeah," she said, "but I see the shrink today. I'm not sure I can handle two sessions in one day." And, with that, she dragged herself into her wheelchair and, without saying another word, slowly wheeled herself toward her room.

She would have another shower, to ease up the soreness; then she had her first session with the shrink. Too bad that session wasn't after lunch. She would need food because she already felt weak. Her body hummed nicely. It was sore but maybe a good sore. Tomorrow she'd be even more so. She'd probably regret having done as much as she had done today. But, as long as Shane seemed to think he knew what he was doing, she'd have to put some trust in him.

So far, he hadn't let her down, and that was more than she could say about a lot of other places she'd been in.

By the time she had a shower and redressed, she was running late for her appointment. Swearing to herself, she rushed as fast as she could toward the office. Then she realized she was likely going in the wrong direction and had to stop and ask someone for directions.

By the time she arrived, she was a good ten minutes late. She knocked on the partially open door, and someone called from inside. Pushing the door wider, she slowly made her way inside to see a woman. Melissa didn't know why she assumed it would be a male. That's what she had had for psychologists up until now. Only after seeing the woman in front of her did she recognize her from her first day's introduction.

Dr. Sullivan looked up, smiled at her, and said, "Hi. It's good to see you again."

"Well, I wasn't in very good shape when you saw me initially." Melissa choked, feeling the need to pull some armor around her from that way-too-searching gaze.

"Arrivals are always tough," Dr. Sullivan said with a nod. "How are you settling in now?"

"I'm settling in," she said. "Still tired, still not quite there yet. But I've recovered from the transfer."

"Good."

At the silence that ensued, Melissa could feel herself tense.

"I gather you're not particularly open to having this visit?"

"Why do you say that?"

"Because you're already guarding against any questions I might ask."

"Well, it's always a bit awkward," she said, "because they never seem to be the questions that I can answer."

"How so?"

"It just seems like, whenever I come to a session like this," she said, "I feel like I'm a student in class still, where I'm searching for the right answer that you want to hear because that's the only way to get a passing grade."

Dr. Sullivan looked at her, then started to chuckle. "*Honesty.* I like that," she said, "and please don't give me answers that you think I want to hear. I would just like to talk to you."

"What do you want to talk to me about?" she asked forcefully. "Because there isn't anything I want to talk about."

"Then let's find something you do want to talk about," she said.

Melissa stared at her nonplussed. "I don't know what that would be."

"Any hobbies?"

"Not anymore," she said. "Not for a long time."

"Why did you join the navy?"

"Because I didn't have a family or a home, only one friend, and I was looking for a way to identify to the world around me."

"Interesting. Why navy? Why not army? Why not air force?"

"I love water," she said with a shrug. "I knew a couple people who were going in, and I thought it was a good idea at the time."

"Any regrets?"

"Nope," she said. "It's just now I feel I'm at a crossroads again, and I don't really have anywhere to go. I have nothing pointing me in a specific direction."

"You're talking about your future?"

"Yes," she said. "It just seems like I've hit the end of the road, and I don't know what's next."

"Do you have to have the answer to that right now?"

"I hope not," she said, "because then it will feel as if I'm already going to fail."

"I don't think failure is really an option here," Dr. Sullivan said a nod. "We're much easier to get along with than that."

"You are. I'm not sure if I am though," Melissa admitted. "It seems like I always expect more out of myself than others do."

"I think that's a common human problem too," she said. "We're always much more critical and harder on ourselves than we are of others. And then we take what other people say and twist it around so it makes it look worse for us. When really the comment was just that, a comment."

"I don't think I have so much that problem," she said, "but I've always had trouble fitting in. Part of the reason why I went into the navy, I think I was looking for that brotherhood we hear so much about. I was looking for a family."

"Did you find it?"

Melissa sat back, wondering at the answer. "I'll say no," she said. "I found a friend group, but they weren't a family."

"And you got along with each other?"

"I think we did fine, but it didn't become that same closeness that I had hoped for."

"Did you see others forming those kinds of groups?"

Melissa nodded emphatically. "That I did," she said. "And again, that left me feeling left out, as if I'd done something wrong, or I wasn't quite enough, or I hadn't quite enough skills or the right personality or something."

"And how did that make you feel?"

"How it makes anybody feel?" she said. "Inadequate."

"Isn't it great how we always judge ourselves by our relationships with others?"

"Is that what we do?" she asked.

"Some of us, yes," Dr. Sullivan said. "If you think about

it, if you had formed that friend group, you would have seen yourself as a success. But because you, in your mind, had something very specific that you could see as being a triumph, yet didn't achieve it, then you felt like you were a failure. And it may not have even been you who was at fault. It may have entirely been that nobody there clicked with you. So it wasn't that you did anything wrong but that the whole scenario wouldn't work, no matter what."

Melissa sat back, wondering. "I guess," she said. "I never thought of it that way."

"And that's all we're doing here," she said. "We're opening up your mind to thinking about things in a different way."

She nodded but didn't say anything, still wondering about her words.

"Do you have any friends who are close?"

"No," she said, "and none from the navy stayed with me. After my accident, it really did feel like I was all alone."

"And you're not the first to say that either because really, when it comes down to it, we're born alone, then we usually die alone. In between, we hit various milestones, and hopefully we will have somebody walk beside us. And sometimes we have to hit those milestones alone. Everybody has trials and tribulations and troubles that they have to deal with, and sometimes just nobody can help you get through it.

"Some people seem to have more of those in a lifetime than is fair, and others seem to have very little. There always seems to be somebody who has a charmed life, and it seems like they always get the best jobs, the best partners, the best of everything, and they didn't do anything to deserve it. Whereas others seem to work and work and work and never get anywhere, even though they try so hard. It's like there is no justice. And sometimes it's got nothing to do with any of it. It's just luck. It's not even fate as much as it's a throw of a card or a roll of the dice."

"It's hard to think that my life became a card toss."

"Nobody wants to think of that. You always want to think that there's a reason for everything, and maybe we just don't know what it is yet," she said with a smile. "How are the pain levels since you arrived?"

"A little rough," she said, "but I'm dealing."

"But that's what you're used to doing, isn't it?" Dr. Sullivan said with a gentle smile.

Melissa nodded slowly. "I guess I am."

"So," Dr. Sullivan said, "when are you going to live, not just deal?"

SHANE STOPPED IN Melissa's room later that afternoon to see how she was doing after their first session. She lay on the bed, facing away from him, still in that same awkward position. He frowned at that. He knocked gently on the door and said, "It's Shane. How are you doing?"

She let her head roll toward him as the rest of her body remained stiff and immobile.

He hated that. The human body was supposed to be fluid. It was supposed to be gentle and moving. It was supposed to shift and bounce as needed. But, in her case, it was like everything was locked down.

She smiled up at him and said, "You worried about me already?"

"I was hoping that today wasn't too hard on you."

"It wasn't," she said, "but I'm definitely feeling it. I can't imagine what tomorrow'll be like."

"How about a hot tub then?"

"But," she said and looked at him. "I thought I wasn't allowed to?"

"Bent the rules. I would not like to have you seize up overnight."

She winced at that. "Me too."

She slowly sat up, and he watched the movement. "You're really favoring that left side."

"Yep," she said, "but that's just part and parcel of it. After being T-boned by a military truck, I'm lucky to be alive. Even knowing it wasn't my fault as he ran a red light doesn't help."

"That's okay," he said, mentally putting something down in his chart about her. As he walked over, he said, "Sit up straight for me, and, as she sat there, he said, "Okay. I'll put some pressure on your hips. I want you to see if that makes it easier or worse for straightening up." And with his gentle hands, he placed them on either side of her lower back and pressed in softly.

She stiffened and straightened up a little bit more. "If I could sit like that," she said, "I'd feel like I was at least sitting straight up."

"You're quite a bit straighter but not straight enough yet," he said. "We have a lot of work to do."

"You keep saying that," she said, "and then, after our first session, you're already worried and want me to go into a hot tub to stop any reaction."

"It just means I care," he said. When an awkward silence followed that, he looked up to see her studying him with a questioning gaze. "Is it wrong to care?"

"No," she said with a shrug. "Just not something I'm used to."

He smiled gently. "Not all the world is a cold, empty, dark place."

Her lips twitched. "Not all of it, no," she said, "just most of it."

He chuckled. "We'll have to work on that belief system of yours too."

"Maybe," she said. "But a hot tub would be nice."

"Did you eat lunch?"

"I did," she said.

"Good," he said. "In that case, let's get you down there."

"Now?"

"Now," he said. "Where's your bathing suit?"

She pointed to the drawer off to the side. He opened it up and pulled out a simple one-piece black suit and said, "You need help getting it on?"

She shook her head. "I can do it."

"Okay," he said. "Get it done now, and I'll take you down myself."

She slowly made her way to the floor, then into the bathroom. It took her a lot longer to get dressed than she had expected, mostly because she was dealing with a bad case of nerves. *Did he care?* Or was that just him talking? Because she hadn't done anything but think about him. She thought it was because of his role in her life, but maybe it was more than that.

She frowned, wondering where all these stupid school-girlish butterflies were coming from. It had been a long time since she'd had a crush on a guy, and no point in having one now, not with the shape she was in. Shane could have his pick of women. He didn't need somebody broken down, like her.

With that thought firmly pushed to the back of her mind, she finished dressing, made her way out to her room again, and said, "Is there a towel or a robe or something?"

"Here," he said, opening another cupboard.

He pulled out a thick fleece, almost a bathrobe, but she figured it was probably for the pool. She put that on atop her bathing suit and sat back down on the wheelchair. "I'm not sure I'm strong enough to make my way there and back again," she warned.

"Well, I'll push you there," he said. "Then we'll see how you do afterward."

"Is this more training?"

"Oh, it's definitely more physio," he said, "but an easier kind."

"If you say so," she said.

When they got down to the hot tub, he locked the wheels on her chair and gave her a hand up, helped her get to her feet and over to the stairs and a railing. As soon as she sat down on the seat in the warm water, she groaned.

"Are you okay?" he asked, kneeling beside her.

She nodded. "Yes. It feels really good." She watched as he took off his shoes and socks, then he sat on the edge beside her, his feet in the water.

He said, "I want you to turn so that you're putting some of those muscles against the jets."

She shifted where he asked and had her lean forward ever-so-slightly, where he slowly worked the long muscles of her shoulders and across her lower back. He worked quietly, just trying to ease the stiffness.

As soon as he was done, he said, "Lift your arms." He checked her balance and her stretching to see if the fingertips were even close to matching, then had her do a few more stretches. He asked, "Now how do you feel?"

She gave a little shake, almost like a puppy wiggle, and looked at him and said, "I feel quite a bit better." She stood up using the handrail and walked across the hot tub, then back toward him again.

He smiled to see her movements much smoother, much less of a crab hobble.

"Things are moving, at least a little bit," she said.

"Looks like they're moving a lot," he said with a gentle smile.

She grinned. "Hey, if I could do this outside of the hot tub, it would be great."

"That's the goal," he said. "Now let's get you back to your room."

"Are you sure I can't stay in here?"

He hesitated, looked at her, and said, "How about for ten minutes, and I'll come back?"

She nodded and sank back against the jets. "And it's okay?" she said. "I mean, if you let me take an extra ten minutes?"

He chuckled and put his shoes and socks on. He headed up to the cafeteria, where he contacted Dennis. "You got any of those ice creams?"

"I've been preparing a flood of ice cream parfaits," he said. "You want one?" He pointed to the side, where Shane could see trays full of the treats.

He snagged two spoons and two parfaits. "Perfect."

"Who's that for?"

"I've got Melissa in the hot tub," he said. "This would be great." He carried them down the stairs toward the hot tub.

She lay there, her long neck gently stretched with her head resting against the back of the hot tub, her body floating upward. He smiled at that because it was one of the best things she could do. Just completely relax, letting the heat work away on her joints, on her sore muscles.

As he approached, she looked up. "Is it that time already?"

"Not quite," he said. He held out an ice cream parfait and said, "How about one of these?"

"Oh my," she said, staring at it. "I love ice cream."

"Well, we don't always get it, but Dennis has been bringing more of it in." He sat down beside her on the dry side and held out the ice cream.

Chapter 6

SEVERAL DAYS WENT by as Melissa settled into a pattern. The next morning she looked at her phone on purpose. She'd been here now ten days. Ten whole days. It had gone by so fast. Even more of a surprise was to see that she was doing okay.

Shane looked at her halfway through one of her sessions and asked, "Problems?"

She shook her head. "No. I'm just shocked that I'm not in any pain."

He looked at her, startled. "Does that mean we aren't working hard enough?"

"Good Lord, no," she said with feeling. "I'm just encouraged."

"Good." And he gave her a quiet smile.

Just something about that smile of his. But she had also come to learn that Shane was extremely well regarded by everybody else in the center, and his time was at a premium. She was honored that Shane was her therapist, and she had better remember not to take his attention as anything other than professional. She hadn't thought she would ever be worried about that, but she didn't appear to be herself these days. As she lay here, he nudged her gently.

"I guess that means you're done, huh?"

She looked at him in surprise. "Sorry. I'm just drifting

off."

"That's why I'm asking," he said with a smile. "It just seems like you're not quite here."

"Well, I need to be," she said, "because, in order to have the progress I want, we need to move this forward a little more."

He nodded. "Good. I'm glad to hear that. Let's get back to work."

When he finally called it quits after another thirty minutes, she lay here on the ground, her chest heaving. "It feels like I have more range of movement in my arms," she said, so pleased, as she stretched her arms overhead and stretched out her hands and feet as far as they could go.

"You do," he said. "There's been a lot of improvement."

"Good," she said. "Definitely room for it."

He laughed at that. "Don't worry," he said. "We have a long way to go yet."

She nodded. "As long as I can see progress, it's so much easier to keep at it. I feel defeated when I can't see any progress."

"Exactly. Not to worry," he said. "You're a long way from hitting your limit," he said. "Do you need a hand up?"

She looked up at him. "No, let me try rolling over." She slowly rolled over, until she was on her hands and knees.

At that, he stopped her. "Now, instead of using the wheelchair for support," he said, as got down beside her, "see if you can move your left leg so your left foot is in front of you for support, then slowly stand up."

It took her a moment, and it wasn't terribly graceful, but she did manage it. She looked at him in surprise. "Not sure I've ever done that before."

"Getting up and down from the ground is a really good

skill to train your body into doing," he said.

She nodded and took the half step toward the wheel-chair, and this time, instead of just plunking herself down, she slowly sat down.

He looked at her with a special smile. "And that's another achievement."

She nodded. "And I felt that one too," she said, "so yay for having enough improvement to feel it." And, with that, she headed out the door.

"Don't forget to keep eating well," he said. "How are the green drinks?"

She looked back at him and frowned. "I haven't had any in a few days."

He looked at her and said, "Did you cancel them?"

"I didn't think they were something I was canceling or approving," she said. "They were just appearing, but I haven't had one recently."

"I'll check into that," he said. "You need them every day."

She wrinkled up her nose.

He laughed and said, "Now, none of that." He walked over, tapped her lightly on the nose, and said, "You need them."

"Okay," she said. "As everything else is moving forward better than I'd expected, I'll trust you on this."

"Do that," he said with a bright smile. "You won't be sorry." At that, he turned and walked out, heading back to his office.

She stared at his back as he left, feeling a heavy sigh releasing from her chest as she wheeled down the hallway.

"What's that for?" Dani asked.

Melissa looked at her friend. "You always seem to pop

up in the most unexpected places."

Dani smiled and said, "Well, I'm all around this place all the time. How are you and Shane getting along?"

Immediately Melissa felt tongue-tied, but she shrugged and, with as much enthusiasm as she could find, said, "Fine."

"Fine?" Dani's gaze was a little more intense than Melissa would have liked.

"Fine," she said. "There's obvious progress, and, for that, I'm delighted."

Dani's eyebrows shot up. "Now that's lovely," she said. "I'm so happy for you."

"Me too," she said. "You forget just how much you stop believing in yourself, until you see some forward movement, and then you wonder how you could have let yourself stop believing."

"I don't think it's as much that you stop believing," Dani said, "as much as you stop thinking about it. And we tend to slide into a negativity versus optimism, so it's like a natural step to go backward."

"It still sucks," Melissa said with a laugh. "But today I managed to do a couple things that I hadn't done before, so it's all good." She slowly wheeled herself toward her room.

"What are you doing now?"

"It's lunchtime," she said, "so I was going to the washroom before the cafeteria."

"Well, if you're up for it," Dani said, "my father is here. He wants to see you."

She looked at her in delight. "The Major's here?"

Dani nodded. "He extended his trip by a few extra days, so he didn't get home as early as expected. But he's back now. I thought maybe if you were up to it,"—and she stopped and looked at her friend—"maybe you could join us for lunch?"

"Absolutely. Does that mean anything different than going to the cafeteria though?"

"Absolutely not," Dani said with a laugh. "You'll see my father as soon as you get there because he'll be holding court, as usual."

"He always was quite the character," she said with a knowing grin.

"Well, that hasn't changed." Dani chuckled. "How about I wait for you?"

Melissa quickly used the washroom and changed into a fresh shirt. "Ready," she said.

As they headed toward the dining room, Dani asked, "How are you doing emotionally here?"

"I'm getting there," she said. "There's a lot of change, a lot of adjustments."

"But all good?" She heard the note of worry in her friend's voice.

Melissa looked up and said, "Dani, you've done a great job here. I can't believe it. What you've created, it's amazing." Dani flushed with pleasure, but Melissa meant it. "Seriously," she said. "I'm not just trying to be a friend. This is amazing. And I haven't had a chance to get down to the animals, except to see the various ones that come through here. But, once I realized you had animals all over the place too, it just made my heart smile."

"The animals are a big hit," Dani admitted. "Not just because animals are here but also because we're helping the animals. And that's a two-pronged benefit for everybody."

"I can't imagine," she said. "I wish I could do something with animals myself. You know that I'd have a hobby farm and half a dozen critters of my own."

"Absolutely," she said. "But you have a lot of abilities, and it's not the time for you to start worrying yet about your future. But keep those ideas in mind. Maybe you can do something with animals."

"Like Aaron?" Melissa teased.

Dani flushed with pleasure. "Like Aaron," she said. "But, in his case, it was something he wanted to do way back when anyway. So this was just him finally aligning his work with what his heart really wanted to do."

"And I imagine that makes a lot of difference."

"I didn't really have any goals when I started out here, except to help my father, but it certainly made a difference now that I do have a purpose in my life."

"I think that's what I'm missing," Melissa said. "I'm still a little lost."

"You're a little lost, but that's because so much in your world needs your focus, but you're getting there. Don't shortchange yourself."

"I hope so," she said. "No," she stopped and shook her head. "No, I know so."

"Good," Dani said, as she led the way to the cafeteria. Even before they arrived, they heard the laughter and a louder noise level than usual. She rolled her eyes. "As you can tell, my dad is here." She chuckled, and they pushed open the door. The din rose and fell as the waves of conversation washed over them. And then Dani called out, "Major."

After a moment of silence, she heard him saying something about having to go, and then he walked toward her. Melissa looked at the big robust man in front of her. "He's not quite the way I expected."

"Well, he's pretty well crashed and burned and been reborn from the inside out," Dani said. "That's why I came here and built this. It was to help him, and it's been a godsend for him."

The Major walked over, took one look at Melissa, and his face split into a huge beaming grin, but it was the gentlest of arms that reached down and gave her a hug. "If it isn't beautiful little Melissa," he said. "I would love to see you any place but in here, but, if you need help, this is where you belong."

Melissa smiled, feeling the tears in the back of her eyes because really, all the years she'd been looking for family, she'd been looking for what Dani had—a father who cared, a parent, somebody who would be there, and the closest Melissa had ever had was the Major. But he wasn't hers; he was Dani's. And something in Melissa's world hadn't allowed her to accept him quite the same way, even though she knew that he'd have been more than welcoming. Only she'd still been dealing with her own hurts at the time.

She smiled up at him and said, "Don't you look fine."

He gave one of his huge belly laughs and said, "I do, indeed. And you can thank my daughter for that. We've been to Hades and back again, but we're here now, and that's where we need to be. And it's a good place to be."

"I'm glad to hear that," she said, "and nobody's more grateful than me. I didn't want to ever be in a position where I needed to come here," she said, "but, now that I am, Dani has welcomed me with open arms."

"Of course she has," he said. "We all would." He looked around and smiled, saying, "I haven't eaten, so what about you? You're here to get food too?"

"I'm hungry," Melissa admitted. "Shane put me through the works this morning."

"I did not," Shane protested from behind her.

She twisted around and smiled up at him, loving the teasing banter from everyone in the place. "Well, let's just say you put me through more than you have so far."

"That's true," he said. "I'll let you get away with that one."

She chuckled and looked up to see the Major, studying her and Shane, a speculative look in his eye. She immediately shook her head. "No, no, no. No, you don't."

He smiled and said, "Be good for you."

"None of that," she warned.

He chuckled, grabbed the handles of her wheelchair, and said, "Food. Let's get food."

"You don't have to look after me," she protested.

"Well, it hasn't been so long that I've forgotten what it's like," he said. "It's not as much of a case of looking after you as helping you. Remember that," he said.

"I'm trying to."

"I remember you always used to be a tough little nut who hated to ask for assistance, who hated to have other people do things for you, feeling like you were supposed to do it all yourself."

"Well," she said hesitatingly, "was I like that even back then? Because that hasn't changed."

"Oh, my goodness, you so were. You had this big shield around you that said, *Stay away, nobody's allowed in.* But Dani and I didn't listen."

Melissa chuckled at that. "No, you didn't." So much affection was in her tone that she realized, of all the things she had missed, it was Dani and the Major.

SHANE WAS INTERESTED to see how Melissa related to Dani and the Major. Particularly the Major. Shane could see the affection in her eyes. And he realized just how much of her issues stemmed from the loss of her parents in her late teens. She'd become very close to Dani at the time, until Melissa had made the decision to join the navy. Her Hathaway House record had multiple notes on the issue, some from Dr. Sullivan as well, and Shane knew that Melissa would have to deal with an awful lot of adjustments and life patterns. Hearing the Major brush aside her protest made Shane feel good to realize the Major had pegged her right.

Dani looked at Shane. "She's a good person," she whispered. "She took a big hit at a young age." Dani explained about the loss of Melissa's parents, how Dani and her father had been as close to Melissa as she would let them get, but the Major had been right. "She forged this big wall, afraid that, you know, anything else happening in her world and she'd break, couldn't handle it. I tried hard not to get her to go into the navy, but she was pretty adamant, and I didn't really have any reason to keep her away from it. I wanted her to stay with us, where she could be with somebody who knew her and cared, but she was determined to move on and to find something else in her life."

"And maybe she just needed to find her own path," Shane said.

Dani nodded. "Look where it left her."

"Yes, but everything for her is fixable," Shane said.

Dani looked at him. "Hopefully. You think she'll come through this okay?"

"Once we can stop the pain that's crippling her all the time. And that's mostly about muscle alignment and some structural stuff. With that alone, she'll be a different person."

Dani beamed and said, "I'll hold you to that."

He laughed. "Well, I'm glad you care so much about her. I get the feeling she really needs that."

"She does, and she also has a hard time asking for it."

"She has a hard time asking for anything, including for me to stop when she's had enough. It is a problem."

"She's always been very stubborn," Dani muttered. "Stubborn, capable, frustratingly independent."

He nodded. "I've seen all that plus," he said with a smile. "And that's all good. She'll need it all. But it's all about having it balanced."

Dani faced him. "That's part of your job, isn't it?"

"It is," he said, "but it sure helps if I have something to work with, instead of something to work against."

Chapter 7

LIFE AT HATHAWAY House was not what Melissa had expected, but it settled into a rhythm faster, smoother, and easier than she thought possible. The days were whipping past, and she was adapting. She looked forward to seeing Dennis every day, and, of course, Shane was the highlight of her day, but she didn't want to tell him that. She knew that she was building up a stupid childhood crush on him, and she would have to get past that real fast.

If anybody in this complex belonged to everybody, it was Shane. Well, maybe Dennis too. Dani and Stan appeared to belong to everybody as well. Stan definitely had a soft spot in everybody's heart. But then he kept bringing up animals that made them all want to take him and the animals home. He'd shown up with two baby squirrels the other day.

They were just old enough to get into mischief, and he'd been hard-pressed to keep the squirrels contained in the little bundle he had them wrapped up in. But she'd loved every minute spent with them. Definitely something she would love to do in the work sector. She was just about to ask Stan about the work involved downstairs, then realized that she was still a long way away from being physically capable of working at all.

She hadn't seen Aaron yet, but apparently he was coming home soon for a visit. He was almost done with the year's schooling; then he'd work downstairs with Stan. She couldn't think of anything better.

Melissa wasn't up for attending a university, not for many years of it at least. But maybe she could do something. She would love to be around the animals, of course, but not just yet. She would first deal with all the things that she still had to work on. But things were getting there. After breakfast, she had her first visit of the week with Dr. Sullivan. As she wheeled in, Dr. Sullivan looked at her and said, "Well, there's a smile on your face."

"There is," she said. "I've been here now three weeks, almost four weeks, and I'm seeing enough progress that I'm feeling good about my decision to come here."

"And what about Dani? Had that friendship worked into your decision-making process?"

"It's nice to see her," she admitted. "I wasn't used to seeing somebody who was so open in her affections before. She and the Major were very foreign to me. My parents, my family? I hadn't realized how stiff and formal my relationship was with them, until I met Dani and her father. Their relationship was so very different, and it was something that I really wanted, but, at the time, it felt like I was being disloyal to my parents, even though they were dead and gone, but it was like having to be true to their memory." She shook her head. "People are really messed up."

"Sometimes when we're in pain," Dr. Sullivan said, "it's hard to see the helping hands being offered, the joy and the hope and the love that's there because we think we don't deserve it, or we shouldn't accept it because it's wrong, or we feel guilty because we're alive, and the people around us are dead, and we don't deserve anything better than that. All of those are normal human emotions, but that doesn't mean that they are ones we should hang on to. You're an adult now. You know so much more about that process and who you were back then, what sent you into the navy, and what has you sitting here now in this position. Now maybe you're ready to accept a little more from Dani and the Major."

"Well, it seems like the Major is still very much the same, maybe even more gregarious," she said. "He still won't take no for an answer."

Dr. Sullivan laughed. "That's hard to imagine, isn't it?" They both chuckled at that.

"He's a very big-hearted person," Melissa said with a smile. "I remember he was always there with a hug, if I needed it. And, of course, back then I desperately needed them, but I also knew that I couldn't depend on them because, well, look what happens when you depend on people."

The doctor nodded and said, "They leave you, don't they?"

She looked up and could feel the tears clogging her throat. "It's stupid because I know my parents didn't want to leave me. They didn't want to die in an accident, but because they did, they left me, and I still hold some of that hurt inside."

"And that's totally normal," she said quietly. "It's very normal, and sometimes people even feel abandoned by the death of another person. It's not that that person would have chosen that exit from our world, but it happened, and you're the one left dealing with the mixed bag of emotions. So, take the time and sort it out, realize that you've let some of that color your world now and stop you and hold you back from having that family you want, having that group of friends you want. It was always there on offer, and it probably was in the navy, but you maybe were still so afraid that you would be the one left behind, that the others would turn around and eventually leave you, that you didn't put any effort into making it happen."

Melissa sat here, staring at her in shock. "Wow," she said. "I hadn't really considered that either."

"Take the time to consider it now," she said. "And just be easier on yourself. Don't judge, accept the emotions, accept all of it for what it is. Give it the honesty to acknowledge that it's there. Then you walk away from it, let it go."

"That's the trick, isn't it?" she said quietly. "To accept it as a nonjudgment."

"Exactly," Dr. Sullivan said. "Relax, love yourself, love what's coming up, and let it go. You'll be a whole new person for it afterward."

SHANE HAPPENED TO be going down the hallway from one of his other sessions, preoccupied with his tablet. Only as he moved to avoid a wheelchair did he note it was Melissa coming out of Dr. Sullivan's office. He stopped, looked at her, and smiled. "Hey," he said. "Sorry, I didn't see you."

"I'm hardly somebody to miss," she said humorously, pointing to the wheelchair.

He shook his head. "Forget about the wheelchair," he said. "You're somebody who's hard to miss anyway." Her smile beamed, and he laughed. "And I meant it."

"Uh-huh," she said, chuckling. "Sure you did."

He shook his head. "You'll have to work on that."

"Work on what?" she asked curiously.

"The inability to accept a compliment for what it is."

She stopped and stared.

He shrugged his massive shoulders. "I meant it," he said. "You're hard to miss." She obviously didn't know what to say, so he smiled and said, "How did your session go?"

"Oh, she's an interesting person to talk to," Melissa admitted. "It's different from what I thought I would be getting out of it. But it's helping."

"Good," he said. "That's important."

"I just didn't realize," she said, as she wheeled down the hallway beside him, "just how much all this interacts with everything else in my system."

"A lot of people like to forget that healing has to happen on all levels," he said in a serious tone. "And sometimes they don't like to have it pointed out. Because a lot of times people come into an injury, an accident, with some really deep grudges, for completely different reasons, different people involved. But it's the same thing. You still have to let go of some of the stuff in order to let your body do what it needs to do."

"That sounds so ... woo-woo*ish*," she said with a laugh. "For want of a better word."

"I know," he said. "But we see it time and time again here."

She nodded. "I guess I just hadn't thought about it before."

"Well, now you have plenty of chances to think about it."

"Which is exactly what these sessions appear to make me do," she admitted.

"Good," he said. And then in a gentler voice, he continued, "Just don't stress yourself too much about it because then you're defeating the purpose."

She rolled her eyes at that. "It's not like there's an easy way to handle any of this."

"Maybe not," he said. "But, when you think about it, there's an awful lot that one can do, and a lot of it is just allowing yourself to heal, allowing yourself to heal inside as well as outside."

She nodded slowly.

He pointed at her room and asked, "Are you going in there or are you heading down to the cafeteria? What's next on your schedule?"

"Well," she said, "I think I have an update meeting with Dani. She said to stop by whenever I had a moment today. Then I'm not sure. I may have an hour or two off this afternoon."

"Wow," he said. "How'd that happen?"

She looked up at him, smiled, and said, "I figured somebody must have dropped the ball."

"Not likely," he said. "Maybe they just knew you needed a break."

"And that's possible," she said. "It is nice, but I'm also at loose ends."

"Why not go down and visit Stan?" he said.

"Can I just go down there though?" she said doubtfully. "I figured I'd be in the way."

"And you'd be wrong there," he said, laughing, "because Stan's always happy to see people."

"Is there anything useful I can do?"

He checked his watch and then, on a sudden decision, said, "Come on. I'll take you down now. We'll see if any animals need feeding or petting and looking after."

She looked up at him, but he could see the pleased grin

on her face and the twinkle in her gaze.

"I'd love to," she confessed, "but I don't want to take you away from work."

"I'm just heading to the office to do paperwork," he said. "I can do that afterward too."

"If you're sure."

He rolled his eyes. "Remember what I said? This is an offer. Accept it and let's go."

And laughing, she wheeled up behind him and said, "If you say so."

"I say so," he said, feeling a certain release and freedom inside.

"Do you ever get to do picnics out here?" she asked, as they went down the elevator.

"I know a lot of patients have," Shane said. "I've thought about it, but I just never made it a priority to try it out. I do come down here in the evenings with a coffee."

"Now that," she said, "would be nice. Just in the evening before bed, maybe for a couple hours—at eight, nine, ten o'clock—when the air is cool and refreshed after a hot day," she said with a nod.

"Exactly." He smiled down at her. "I like to hit the pool around then too."

"Ah," she said. "The joys of not being a patient."

"If there's something you want or need," he said, "you have to speak up. We can't read minds."

She looked at him and said, "I doubt I'd be allowed to go to the pool at that hour, would I?"

He thought about it. "It depends on whether anybody's there for you," he said. "Any patient's at the pool must have somebody watch over them. In the evenings it's open to everybody, but, if a patient wants to go, we still have to ensure somebody can keep an eye on them, just for safety."

"Which basically means," she said, "that I can't go."

"I'm not sure about that," he said, shaking his head. "Again, you're jumping to an assumption that I'm not sure is true."

"Well, maybe you could find out for me," she said impulsively. "I know, in the evening sometimes, it would be lovely to get out and just ease back in the pool after a hot day."

"Depends on how tired you are at night too," he murmured.

She nodded. "I haven't been sleeping all that great, so that might make it better."

"We could try it. Just let me know, as I usually hit the pool every night."

At that, he walked out of the elevator and pointed toward the double doors for the vet clinic. "These doors are automatic, specifically for the wheelchairs. And for people carrying animals," he added as an afterthought.

"We always like to think that everything's here for us, don't we?" she said. "When really it's probably about the people bringing in animals."

He chuckled and said, "You know what? I never even thought about it. I assumed it was here because of the human patients, but you could be right."

As they walked in, Robin stood at the desk. She looked up with a big smile. "Hey, Shane, what's up?"

He smiled and introduced Melissa.

Robin came around from behind the counter. "Hi. Welcome to Hathaway House and the animal section," she said with a chuckle.

"You're lucky to work here," Melissa said. "I met Hoppers the other day with Stan," she said, "and it reminded me just how much I miss animals in my life."

"Well, you can sign up for an animal tech course," she said. "It doesn't take all that long, and you could always look at adding animals back into your life, but it's not all sun and roses."

"No," she said. "A lot of death is here too, isn't there?"

"There can be, but there's an awful lot of reward. So I certainly wouldn't want to discourage you from getting into the field." She looked at Shane. "Depending on what your injuries are all about." She added, "It's something that you could certainly look at, and Shane would definitely help you get back into shape, so you can handle whatever physical effort was required."

She looked at Robin in surprise. "Sounds like you have a lot to do with Shane and the people upstairs."

"Well, my partner was a patient upstairs," she said, "and my brother is currently there."

At that, Shane remembered Keith. "I keep forgetting that," he said. "Between Keith and Iain, you're having quite the relationships here, aren't you?"

"And I love it," Robin said. "It makes me feel very connected to everybody."

"And I think that's what I'm missing," Melissa said quietly, as she sat at Shane's side.

Shane looked at her. "What? What is it you're missing?"

"That connection," she said, "that sense of belonging. It's been missing a long, long time in my world."

Robin leaned on the desk and studied her for a long moment. "You know it's not from the outside, right? It's from the inside."

Chapter 8

MELISSA LOOKED AT her. "That sense of belonging?"

"I had a similar thing with a rough childhood," she said. "Some ... family issues. But I found that, for me—and I mean, obviously I can only speak for myself—but having a sense of connection to myself, the acceptance of who I was, where I was, what I was doing, made a big difference. And, coming from that point, I could then reach outward with the same sense of acceptance, and I found that people were there for me more than I thought. I had assumed they weren't there for me because I couldn't really see it, I couldn't see myself."

Shane piped up, "Wow, that's a really good insight. I'm not sure too many people will have had that experience and come out with the same wisdom."

"No," Robin said. "It's been a really good thing to have my brother Keith here," she said, "because it's helped us to work through a few of our own family issues. I love him dearly, but we needed to talk about things." She shrugged. "We didn't have an easy time growing up. Keith had the worst time of it," she said. "This time, it's helping us pull together. And, of course, Iain is a huge help in that way too."

Shane nodded. "Iain has done a phenomenal job here," he said warmly. "And the two of you are great together."

She smiled. "Thank you. And you're right. We worked

really hard to be where we're at. It's just so wonderful to have found each other."

"Is there a trick to that self-acceptance?" Melissa asked, Robin's words kept going over and over in her head. "Because it feels like something is very momentous in that, in what you just said."

"Well, if there is," Robin said, "give yourself some quiet time to just think it over, to see what pops up. Don't work on it. It's not homework. It's not something that you have to do. Allow yourself to ponder those issues and to see what comes up."

Melissa nodded. "That seems to be one of the tricks," she said. "You know how there's always that feeling that you're supposed to be doing more, that you're supposed to be trying harder, that you should have all the answers? Instead I feel like I have no answers."

"And instead it's more about accepting that this is where you're at, that this is what you're doing, and that the truth will find its way toward you."

"Exactly," Shane said. "And we don't want to get esoteric about it all, but, at the same time, it's an inner knowing, it's finding out who you are, who'll show up every day for the job, and what a job you'll put in," he said gently.

Melissa smiled. "You always have such great words of wisdom. Is it something to do with being here?"

Robin said, "You know what? Sometimes I wonder. I've become very empathetic, much more intuitive being here, with the relationships, with the people all around me. Everybody is so very caring, and you can see when and where there's a problem. We may not always know how to handle it, but you know enough to back away and to let some people find their way on their own. Like I said, there's a lot of good things to being here." Just then the buzzer on her desk rang. She smiled and said, "I have to get back to work."

"Wait. Before you go," Shane said, "we were just taking a moment and showing her some of the animals around here. Do you have anybody that needs a cuddle?"

"Oh, do we ever," she said. "I'll be back in a minute." With that, Robin disappeared into the back.

Melissa looked up at Shane. "I find the conversations around here so very unique," she said.

"That's because we're all involved in healing," he said, his tone more serious than she'd heard it before. "And, when you think about it, that's so much of what our world is. It's all about healing. It's all about what's the next step for everybody. And that healing rubs off on those of us who work here too. It's not like we're completely immune to it or that we don't have any work to do on ourselves. It's just we don't think we do because we're not in that world. And then, when we are in this world," he said, "it just … it sneaks up on you, and it makes you realize that you have this issue or that issue, and you need to work on it. Growth happens exponentially when it's around another person who's growing."

"And I like that idea," she said. "I was thinking before I got here that I was a huge mess, but maybe I'm not all that bad off."

"Oh my," he said, "you're not bad off at all. And you're doing a wonderful job. You need to give yourself credit for that."

"Am I?"

He stopped and looked at her, then nodded very seriously. "Absolutely," he said. "You are doing a great job. You just need to realize that the inside growth is not something that anybody else can measure. Only you can."

And, with that, Robin returned. In her arms was a huge cat. Melissa looked at her and laughed. "Well, I'd say it's a cat because it has the look of a cat, but it's a monster size."

"It's a purebred Maine coon," she said, "and he is huge." The cat just draped in her arms, like a piece of dough, sagging on both sides.

Melissa immediately held out her arms. "Is he friendly?"

"Yep, he's here several times a year for basic shots and toenail clippings, things like that," she said. "The owner said that she'd be here this morning but then phoned to say she couldn't get in 'til the end of the day. So this guy—whose name is Timmy, by the way—was feeling caged, so we brought him out to give him some space." She dropped him gently into Melissa's arms.

Melissa immediately hugged him close. The cat looked up at her, rubbed his face against hers, and a massive diesel engine kicked in. "Oh my," she gasped. "He's gorgeous." She nuzzled her cheek against the cat, who just seemed unable to get enough, and she scratched the back of his head and along his neck. She sat here, enraptured, just loving the feel of this cat that had absolutely no intention of going anywhere, as long as there were humans to look after him. "He is just beautiful."

"Yep, he is. We get a lot of really cool animals in here," she said with a smile.

Melissa looked up at Shane. "Did you want to hold him?"

"No, thanks," he said. "It's all good." He pulled out his cell phone. "Do you mind if I take a picture?"

"Sure, I'd love to have one too," she said.

He took several photos of her holding Timmy, and reluctantly, when Timmy looked like he wanted to check out the reception room, she handed him back awkwardly to Robin, who snagged him up. "That's it, Timmy. Back inside with you now." She carried him to his cage.

Sad, and yet at the same time feeling almost awestruck with the one-on-one meeting, Melissa said, "I should ask Dani about visiting with some of the animals," she said. "I feel like I need to do more of that."

"I'm sure you do," he said. "Do you want to go outside now or go back upstairs?"

"I think I'd like to go outside," she said impulsively. She stopped and looked up at him. "I'm not trying to take you away from your work though."

"Don't worry about it," he said. "As I said, I've got some time."

She smiled. "And it's nice to spend it with you, not in a gym where I'm getting reamed out for not working hard enough." She chuckled.

"That's the job," he said. "This is completely different."

She smiled. "And I like that," she said. "It's nice to see people on a personal level too."

"For us too," he said. "Remember that we live here, and we work here. But we also must have relationships and meet people here on their level as well."

"It's hard to even imagine," she said. "I'm here because of the ... the condition I'm in. But you're here by choice."

"All of us are," he said. "There's work in other places in the country, if we didn't want to be here. But most of us love it and love just helping the people who we have here. It's a very special place."

"And again, kudos to Dani for pulling it together."

"Absolutely. She's done a bang-up job on it. And we all

appreciate it."

"I'm not at all surprised to hear that," she said. "I'm really proud of her."

"Then tell her that," he said.

"I think we all forget to give kudos where kudos belong." She smiled. "Another one of those hard-learned lessons, isn't it? We tend to get so wrapped up in ourselves, we forget that other people have needs and insecurities too."

As soon as they went outside and down the pathway, she stopped almost in her tracks and said, "And there are the horses," she said, shaking her head. "So beautiful just to even see them from a distance."

"Do you ride?"

"No. Never really had the opportunity. They're so big too," she said with a laugh. "Not scared of them though, I'm just … in awe."

"*In awe* is a good way to put it," he said, "because they are very special, but they are certainly not an animal that you want to be too complacent about. It's easy to get hurt just out of ignorance."

"I wouldn't want to hurt them either," she said, "and it feels like I would end up startling them and causing more problems."

"Possibly," he said, "I'm not sure how much of an issue that is though."

"I don't know. They are just lovely to see."

They wheeled down the path, the two of them together, quiet, peaceful. He asked out of the blue, "Do you have anybody waiting for you at home?"

"I haven't had anybody waiting for me in a long time." She wanted to joke about it but knew it wasn't a joking matter. "It seems like I've been alone for a lot longer than I even thought possible."

"Did it bother you to be alone?" he asked curiously.

"No. I didn't really notice it, until I started recovering from all this, and, at one point in time, I wondered what I was recovering for. It was hard to admit, especially to ..."

"To yourself," he said instantly. "Recovery should always be about you. Every decision in life should be about you," he said, "because, if the other person leaves, you've got to be sure that that decision you made is one you can still live with."

"And I've thought about that," she said. "But, no, there isn't anybody." As they strolled along the pathway, she asked, "What about you?"

"No. A lot of relationships are happening here," he said. "So it's been something that I've been thinking about a little bit lately, just because I've watched as there didn't appear to be any relationships, then all of a sudden a good dozen were coming together out of the blue."

"That's lovely," she said.

"It absolutely is," he said. "But it was also unexpected. So it's made me do a little self-analysis, figuring out what it is I want."

"And that can't be easy. You spend all your life helping people," she said. "What do you do to help yourself?"

He chuckled. "I haven't been doing very much at all," he said. "I've been burying myself in work, helping as many people as I can. So maybe it's something I need to look at. I'm not avoiding relationships but haven't left a whole lot of room for one either."

"And maybe it's something you need to just let go and let happen," she said with a cheeky smile.

As it was a repeat of earlier words spoken, he immediately caught her intention and laughed. "Very true," he said. "Very, very true."

The next half hour they spent in peace, as they watched the animals and talked about all things minor. But it was also a milestone that she felt was important, something so very personal and private, almost intimate, about the two of them as they moved outside.

Finally he looked at his watch and, with a heavy sigh, said, "I have to head back. Do you want to come back with me, and I'll make sure you get there safely, or are you okay out here on your own?"

"Well, I'd like to say I'm okay on my own," she said, "but that pathway has a bit of an incline to it."

He chuckled. "There absolutely is. Why don't I escort you to the main grounds, and then you can go where you want to from there."

As soon as they got to the pool area, she said, "If you want, you can leave me here," she said. "I think I'd like to just sit and enjoy the sunshine for a bit."

"Perfect," he said. "Just remember not to get sunburned." And, with that, he gave her a quick smile and disappeared.

SHANE HEADED BACK to his office, knowing he had spent way too much time with her than he should have, but it was hard not to. Something was very special about her that brought out the protectiveness in him, and whether that was good or not, he wouldn't analyze it. It was just nice to think about her on a completely different level than as a patient. Something about her just brought out a completely different set of feelings inside him. And it was about time.

He smiled as he headed to his office.

The smile was instantly caught by Dani, walking down the hallway. "Wow," she said. "Wonder what woman put that smile on your face?"

He stopped, looked at her, and said, "What?"

She burst out laughing. "Just teasing you," she said, "but obviously someone has put that smile on your face."

"Yes," he said. "I was just outside, showing Melissa the animals, and we went for a walk up and down on the pathway."

"Perfect," she said with a cheeky smile. "Sounds like you two are getting along famously."

"She's lovely," he said, "and obviously has been through a lot in her life."

"She has, but more than anything," Dani said quietly, "it's made her more isolated and fearful of getting hurt again."

"I think almost everybody who's been through some relationship trauma, whether it's a death, a loss, or abusiveness," he said, "it's a similar issue, isn't it?"

"It is, indeed," she said. She walked past him, heading to her office, and said, "But as long as she's putting that smile on your face, I'm all for it."

In his office, he sat down, wondering at her words. He didn't look any different, but he felt different. And, with that same smile on his face, he got to work.

As Shane headed down to the hot tub with Keith at the end of the day—to work on some of his sore muscles that he still struggled to control—Shane wondered where and how long Melissa had stayed out in the sun. He hoped not too long because her skin was supersensitive, being as fair as she was. He looked when they arrived at the pool, thankful she wasn't here. He would have felt guilty for leaving her here when he should have taken her up himself.

"You seem distracted," Keith said, looking up at him. "Something wrong?"

"Not at all," Shane said. "I had a patient out here earlier. Just making sure that she's not still here."

"I guess it's hard to turn off, isn't it?" Keith asked.

"It can be," he said. "You know how we invest in you guys. We invest our hearts, our hopes, our energies to try and get you as good as we can, and we don't want to see anything happen to derail your success."

"What about emotionally?" he asked. "Now that I've found somebody, which I still don't quite believe, how do you handle relationships here?"

"Well, it hasn't been an issue before," he said. "It might be now though."

"Ah-ha," Keith said with a chuckle. "It's nice to see that it's not just me who got caught."

"I'm not sure exactly what it is," Shane admitted, "but I'm definitely interested in someone."

"Good," he said. "In that case, you should go after it, if that's what you want."

"Oh, she's not ready," he said.

"You know what? That's what I thought about me, but I was wrong too."

"You think so?"

"Absolutely. Being here, the things we've been through, it's not a case of not being ready. It's not a case of needing more time. It's usually that most of us don't even see what's in front of us. We don't think it's possible. We don't see that relationship or that anybody will even want us. And that's something that I had to get past."

"But you did get past it," he said.

"I did. It took a bit, and that's only down to Ilse that I made it that far," he said, chuckling. "She's been very, very good for me."

"You two do look great together," he said.

"I appreciate that. I still worry that I might be a burden for her, and I know, if she ever heard me say that, she'd trounce me hard for it," he said, chuckling. "And now that I'm getting so much better, and I can see that the improvements will continue, it's just that much easier to move forward."

"While I would have said that this person wasn't quite ready, I think she's also slowly learning a little more about herself, what she wants in life, and … where some of her issues are coming from."

"And that's what life's all about here, isn't it? Every day is some emotional challenge just to figure out what and where people are working from, what the reasons are why they're struggling," he said. "And it's usually not the reason we think it is." He looked up at him. "In your case, you're probably afraid to have a relationship with anybody in case you think, … they think, … it's a patient-therapist-transfer notion. Which I presume the person you're talking about, from what you said, is a patient?"

Shane nodded slowly. "It's because of that issue that personal relationships with patients are always avoided."

"Sounds like that's something that you might need to deal with," Keith said.

"I don't think it's an issue, a situation I have come up against before, but it's unique. And I'll just have to work my way through to accepting that this is potentially my new normal."

Chapter 9

SOMETHING BETWEEN MELISSA and Shane had shifted in a good way. The next few days the smiles were brighter, the touches held longer, and the need to spend more time together deepened. It was a wonderful feeling. They met for breakfast several times a week when before they might have met only once a week. And now they met for lunch every day. She knew other people were commenting, as there were smiles and nods in their general direction when they went in for lunch that following Friday.

She smiled and said, "We're attracting attention."

"Let them comment," Shane said comfortably. "All in all, I would say everybody's pretty happy. At least I haven't heard anything otherwise."

"As long as you don't mind."

"And I'm certainly not against it," he said, chuckling. "And we have to expect a certain amount of interest when you start a relationship."

At his words, she smiled and said, "Here I thought we were past just starting."

"Relationships here develop differently," he admitted. "We're already past so much of the social niceties that people would put on when you first meet. It's different here. There's no energy for that surface level. We are already down to the nitty-gritty of our inner selves here."

"I guess it gets right down to the heart of what really matters, doesn't it?"

They were sitting outside on the deck, both with lunch. She had chosen pasta, whereas he had some Chinese dish.

He nodded. "Here you're already dealing with really deep issues. You're dealing with healing, with the reality of what your current world looks like," he said. "And that means all that other stuff—how you look, how you present yourself—changes. It's different from just putting on makeup and going out to a dance, where you get to be somebody else for a night, and it takes time to get to know who people really are. Here, right now, we know who people are. We see it in our work, on a day-to-day basis."

"I never thought of that," she said, "but it's true. An interesting way to look at life too."

"And it's real," he said. "I think that's why so many of the relationships that have developed here have done so well."

"Well, it gives me hope then," she said with a cheeky smile.

He grinned at her. "The thing is, you need to make sure that whatever is going on between us doesn't negatively impact whatever it is that you need to do for your health, physically and emotionally," he said. "So if you ever find me getting in the way, tell me to butt out."

She chuckled. "If anything, you're showing me that something normal is possible."

"Of course it's possible." Then he smiled. "But that's one of the realizations that you had to come to. That's part of the whole growth process."

"And that's not an easy process to get to," she said, "because, as the patient going through all this, I don't see it. I don't realize that it's a milestone. I'm just focused on working forward until it hits me, and I realize that I've crossed it."

"And I think that's why so many of us can't really tell you what it is you need to do to heal, outside of giving you general guidelines, because that milepost, that realization, is different for every person."

"I guess I just hadn't even considered it," she said honestly.

"Well, now you have," he said with a smile. "So life is … good. You can work toward the next milestone."

She rolled her eyes at that. "Can't imagine how many milestones we'll have to work toward."

"In some cases, there are a lot," he said. "But I can tell you, it's worth it. Every single day, it's worth it."

And she thought about his words for the next week, as it seemed like their friendship deepened, and people around them started to see them as a couple. And something was very special about that. The world was built for couples, as if a bubble were around them. And nobody else seemed to matter. She didn't know for sure that she was falling in love, but she was definitely experiencing feelings for him that she hadn't expected. At breakfast that following Wednesday, they were eating together. Several people were whispering about them a few tables over.

She dropped her gaze to her plate.

"Problems?" he asked, in that very perceptive tone of his.

She smiled. "I'm just … I'm unfamiliar with this," she said.

"Does the talk bother you?" he asked, his gaze searching hers.

"No, not so much that it bothers me," she said. "I wasn't

expecting it, and I'm not used to it, but I can't say that it's a problem. I don't know if it's a problem."

"Right," he said. "Why don't we just take it as not a problem, and we'll carry on."

She smiled. "Like, not borrow trouble before it happens?"

"Exactly." He nodded.

She laughed. "Sounds good. I have a session this morning with the doctors to see how my last set of tests were."

"Good," he said. "You're showing a lot of improvement physically."

"Not enough to walk normally though," she said. "I mean, obviously I can walk-walk, but it'd be nice to not lurch."

"I know what you mean," he said. "I'll show you how much you've improved in our next session." He checked his watch. "And that's in about two hours."

"It is," she said. "I'll head back and get ready for my doctor's appointment."

"Until then," he said, lifting a hand.

She pushed her wheelchair back and turned, heading out. She knew his gaze was on her as she left, she could just feel it. It was that inner knowing. But it was also special too. She was a little afraid to believe in him. In them. He could have anyone he wanted. Why her? Maybe the need to walk normally was more for him to see her as somebody who had done as well as everybody else in here.

As she headed out the doctor's door, after her session, she turned to him. "Oh, I wanted to ask you about walking."

"Well, you are ambulatory, aren't you?" he asked.

She motioned at the wheelchair and said, "Well, I can walk without it, yes. But it tires me out, and physically I'm not very strong to keep it up."

"Have you asked Shane about that?"

"Not yet," she said. "I have a session with him now."

"Well, maybe work on focusing on that," he said. "No reason you can't walk now. You've come a long way. You're not in anywhere near the pain you were in, are you?"

She shook her head, surprised at that. "It's a funny thing about something that's negative," she said. "Because, when you take it away, you tend to forget that it's not there anymore. Because I can focus on so much else. I had forgotten that the pain was as crazy debilitating bad as it was when I first arrived. But you're right, it's much better now."

"So the next step would be to get you walking as efficiently and as cleanly as you can," he said with a bright smile. "You may want to try crutches, but maybe you don't need to because it's not like you can't hold your weight. It's a matter of walking straight and not favoring certain body parts, and Shane is a specialist at that."

She was surprised at his words, and she pondered them as she headed toward Shane and her session with him. As she wheeled in, she said, "I didn't know you were a specialist in walking."

He looked at her and frowned. "Not sure I understand what the comment means."

She explained what the doctor had said.

He laughed. "Well, I'm a specialist in structural integrity, and that's definitely one of the things that we've been working on. That's why you're in much less pain."

"Ah. Well," she said, "according to him I should talk to you about focusing on walking better."

"I was just looking at your test results to see how you're doing," he said. "So we'll go back to having you on the floor and make you do the same exercises that you did day one, then getting down to the floor and back up again. We'll take a look at how that compares to when you first got here. This will be like your midpoint. Then we'll start working on getting your walking stronger."

"I would love to walk into the dining room, pick up my tray, and walk to the table, without it being like this half-crab-hop."

He nodded. "That will definitely be a priority as we push forward now," he said. "But first let's go through what I just suggested," he said. "Push your wheelchair over there, and go lie down on the floor, and I'll take a video as you do it."

She remembered that scenario from the first time. "That was pretty ugly."

"It was," he said, "but you've come a long way since then. I think it's important for you to see exactly how far you've come."

Obediently she followed through on what he asked, and by the time he said, "Okay, that's good," she relaxed on the mat.

He came over to her area with his camera and plugged it into his laptop. "In a second, I'll show you the original video. Then I'll show you the new one."

"Do you want me to come over there?"

"Sure," he said.

She made her way up into the wheelchair, sat on the edge, and watched as he brought up the original video. She had tears in her eyes when he stopped playing it.

He looked at her and asked, "Why the tears?"

"Because I'd forgotten," she said. "The progress has been so slow that I hadn't seen it. But I had forgotten how bad it was."

"Well, now that that video is fresh in your memory," he said, "watch this." He showed her the video of how she had just laid down on the mat and then gotten back up.

She stared in shock. "Wow," she said. "I really hadn't seen any improvement to be that extreme."

"It is extreme," he said. "And it's lovely to see."

She nodded slowly. "I just hadn't realized ..." She broke off, not knowing what to say.

"And now," he said, "we'll take the next step. We'll work on your walking. Instead of the floor work, I want you to stand up against the wall. Heels back, arms at your side, head back."

She got up from the wheelchair, walked a little awkwardly to the wall.

"Now tell me where the pain is."

She immediately put her hand on her lower left side and said, "On the left, a bit higher up, as I'm struggling a little bit too."

"Okay, relax again. How about the head, the neck, shoulders?" he asked. "You should have all this in alignment." He stepped her away from the wall to stand in front of the mirror. "I want you to take a deep breath, to imagine that your chest is like a box. Your shoulders and collarbone are the top of the box, and your head is the handle. And, when you take a deep breath, I want that lid to come off, and I want the handle to come up."

She took a slow, deep breath, mentally visualizing everything he said, and then released it.

"Do that several more times," he said.

When she was done, she said, "That feels weird."

"It does, but you have to get the air all through your

lungs and start to straighten up that chest."

"What does the chest have to do with walking on my feet?"

"Well, the feet are a problem all on their own," he said, laughing. "And we'll start with the feet, and then we have to make sure the hips are in the right alignment. But you also have to be breathing properly." And he did something else. "I want you to lie down. I'll work on your ankles a little bit."

She lay down, and he quickly worked on some of her joints, and the muscles around the joints, and then he gave her a hand back up. "I want you to take a few steps."

She took a few steps, feeling her body shifting, almost as if uncoordinated, as it settled into what the new placement of her feet were. And then she turned around and slowly walked back. "It feels a whole lot better already," she said. "Why didn't we do this at the beginning?"

"You weren't quite ready," he said. "I had today scheduled for a new video to check to see what was next to work on. And obviously what we'll work on is keeping your posture straight and building up these muscles so that you can walk farther and farther. From here on in, I want you to make sure that you walk every day. It's okay to take it slow, to walk slowly as you gain strength. You can even use one crutch if you feel you need the extra support. But I want you to remember a couple of these lessons as we work through them today, so that you can practice them when you're back in your room."

"So, am I supposed to walk into the dining room tonight this way?"

"It would be good if you did, yes," he said, studying her face.

She winced. "And what if I fall and wipe out because I

can't stand straight?"

"I think you'll be surprised," he said. "If you want, I'll meet you there, and we'll see how it is together."

She smiled. "It's like you're becoming my crutch," she said teasingly.

"Well, I wouldn't want to be a crutch, because that's something that you lean on," he said. "It would be much better if I was the one who's there, someone you know you can count on."

She stopped, looked at him in amazement, and said, "Oh, I like that. I really like that."

The trouble was, when it came time that evening to walk to dinner, she was a little tired, a little worried, struggling with her breathing, as she took several steps forward. By the time she made it to the dining room, she pulled up against the doorjamb and just leaned against it for a few minutes. It wasn't that she was tired, but she wanted to walk in okay and not get jostled or bounced by other people. Just then she looked over to see Dani coming up beside her.

Dani smiled and said, "It's good to see you on your feet."

Her voice was so warm and held such admiration in it that Melissa immediately felt like confessing. "I'm leaning here," she said, "because I'm afraid I'll fall down."

"Are you sure?" Dani asked quietly, her gaze twinkling. "Or is it because you're afraid you'll look a fool?"

Melissa wrinkled her nose up at that. "It's that obvious, huh?"

"You've no idea how many people have stood in this exact same place, whether on crutches, in a wheelchair, or on their own two feet, because they were afraid to either make a fool of themselves or just completely fail at something so simple as getting a meal," she said. "There is no failure here. Remember that." And, with that, she walked ahead of her.

Shane's warm voice behind her made her feel even better. "It's good to see you standing. Dani was right. There is no failure here," he said. He held out his arm, as if they were on a date, and said, "Shall we go in for dinner?"

She laughed in delight, slipped her arm through his, and said, "Do I get to use you for support, if I need it?"

"Absolutely, if you need it," he said, "but you won't."

And they moved slowly forward, grateful that the line was moving to the point that, when they got up to where Dennis stood, a huge grin on his face as he saw her on her feet, that she felt like she had the whole world in front of her.

"Don't you look lovely," Dennis said, with a beaming smile.

"What? I didn't look lovely sitting down?"

He laughed and laughed, making her chuckle. "It's good to see a sense of humor too," he said. "Remember. Life isn't about always having a success. Life is always about making every day better than the one before. We often wake up in the morning and think absolutely nothing is good in our world, but it's all about making it through anyway and making something good about it. So, it is lovely to see you. Now what can I get you for food?"

With the two of them together and their meals sitting in front of them, she grabbed her tray and said to Shane, "Well, here goes nothing."

"You'll be fine."

He led the way to a table in a route that was open and wide, and she slowly followed, working carefully on placing her feet properly and keeping her body upright. It's not that she wouldn't fall, but she was afraid she'd immediately revert to that hunchback-crab walk that she'd been doing.

But she made it to the table, even managed to bend down and place the tray carefully before sitting down. As soon as she sat down, she wanted to *whoop* with joy. She said, "I know it's silly, and I know it's crazy, but it feels so good."

"Of course it does," he said. He leaned over, picked up his water glass, and said, "Cheers."

She chuckled and clinked her glass to his and said, "I can't believe I've made it this far."

"And this is still just part of it," he said. "We have lots more to go."

"I know," she said with the gentlest of smiles. "But I have so much to thank you for already." She could sense him withdrawing slightly, and she shook her head. "I don't know what I just said, but you're stepping back."

He looked at her and nodded. "It's one of the things that we always have to watch out for. Gratitude is lovely, and thank you," he said, "but remember. You're the one who's done this, not me."

"What do you mean, *it's something you have to watch for?*"

"It's about making sure you don't mistake other feelings for being grateful."

And then she realized what he was trying to say. "Absolutely not," she gasped. "Oh my," she said. "I can see how that would be an issue, but it isn't for me."

He studied her carefully.

She smiled and said, "I mean it. What I feel for you is not at all connected to gratitude. Of course I'm grateful. You've shown me a whole new way to live. You've helped me get from where I was to where I am, and I know I still have a lot more healing to go."

He said, "And I'm happy to do it because now you can see that the journey is of value. It's funny how many people need proof."

"Well, it's easier with measurable, tangible proof, isn't it?" she said. "We don't have to go on blind faith."

"True enough," he said, and he started eating.

She leaned forward and said, "And that doesn't change the fact that this isn't all about gratitude."

He looked up, gave her a flashing bright smile, and said, "Good," and then he returned to eating.

Feeling like she'd probably said enough—but maybe not enough to satisfy him—still not quite sure what else to do, she started in on her meal too. In the back of her mind she worried. It wasn't just gratitude, was it? Surely not. But she didn't have enough practice or experience in relationships to really understand, and so much was new in her mind-set. So much was new in the way that she looked at the world, as she'd understood how she'd been searching for a way to belong all this time.

She didn't want that to be a reason behind a relationship with Shane. The fact that he could see past her broken body was amazing in itself. But what was it that she was seeing when she looked at him? And it was a question that bothered her for a long time.

Days went by, and those thoughts still sat there in the back of her mind. She kept hoping for enlightenment, but, so far, just all these questions built up.

SHANE WATCHED HER behavior. It wasn't that she withdrew, but it was obvious that she was thinking hard. And that was a good thing. He didn't know if it was his words. He suspected so, but then an awful lot of work was being done behind the scenes with Dr. Sullivan, and he could champion that more than anything because it was so important for Melissa to do that work. She was a wonderful person. He was becoming more attached than he cared to, especially if it ended up being something that wouldn't move forward.

Dani caught him frowning one day and asked, "Problems in paradise?"

He looked up at her and smiled. "How do you know when paradise is right?"

She leaned against the doorframe, her arms across her chest. "You know? I think you go through this uncertainty. This feeling of *Is it right? Is it wrong? Is it for real? Do they care? Do they not care? Is it enough?* And then," she said, "you come out the other side, and there's this feeling of *I know it's right.*" She continued, "It comes from deep inside. It's a feeling of *This is the person I want to be with. This is the person I want to spend time with. This is the person I didn't know I'd been waiting for all this time. This is the person who makes me better,*" she said with a gentle smile. "What you're going through is normal. It's proper. It's correct. It's what you should be going through. And, when you come out on the other side, you will have that sense of having been through the worst, and you'll know deep inside that it's right."

"What if I don't go through that?"

She laughed out loud. "But you are going through that," she said. "You're going through it right now."

He nodded moodily, as he picked up his laptop and disconnected the charging cable from it and packed it up. "I'm not sure that she sees me the way she would see another male."

"Back to that gratitude stuff?"

"I think so," he said. "We talked about it. I'm not sure there's really an answer for it, but it's just something that I've been a little concerned about."

"And that's okay," she said gently. "I understand that. It can't be all that easy, if you're afraid it's not going anywhere. But, from what I've seen, there's certainly an awful lot there for you to work with."

"There is," he said. "Maybe I'm just being impatient."

"Well, that is one thing," she said. "You cannot rush this process, and you can't rush it for her either. She has to come to that same awareness in her own time frame."

"And waiting sucks," he said forcefully.

She burst out laughing. "It so does, doesn't it? Hardly fair at all."

"Not fair at all," he said with a shake of his head. "Still, it is what it is, and that's all fine and good. I promise I'll give her the time she needs."

She laughed. "Glad to hear that," she said in a teasing voice. "I'm also happy to know that you care enough to wait for her."

"It's just … I hate the doubts."

"And that's only because you're in the process," she said, "and it's lovely to see."

He stared at her in outrage. "It's lovely to see me all churned up like this?"

"Well, that's not quite what I meant," she said with a girlish giggle. "But you know what? I'm not totally against it."

He rolled his eyes at her. "That's just mean."

"No," she said with a gentle smile. "That's love."

"It sucks," he said, calling out as she walked away. But her only answer was that lovely peal of laughter. And he grinned, fully aware that everybody in the place was watching his relationship with Melissa, seeing if it would go the way of all the other relationships. He wanted it to, but Dani was once again right. It had to work its way through in its own time frame; otherwise he would feel like he'd cheated Melissa and maybe rushed her.

And that wasn't what he wanted either. He wanted her to be fully aware, fully happy to be with him as he was to be with her. He'd already asked himself the deep questions about whether he could handle somebody who could have an extreme physical disability all her life, and his only answer had been: *Who was better qualified than him? As long as his heart was engaged, he didn't give a hoot about the rest.* She was beautiful inside and out, and her body wasn't an issue. It was about the soul on the inside.

But somehow he had to convince her of that. And that wouldn't be easy. It's not that she was against it; she was just not 100 percent for it yet. And, as much as he wanted to give her time, he was the impatient sort, and he wanted things a little bit more locked down than they were, and somehow he was supposed to wait to make that happen. And that sucked.

Chapter 10

SEVERAL DAYS LATER, it felt like a week later, Stan came up to Melissa with a tiny dog sporting a tiny set of wheels on his back end. "Have you met Chickie?"

"Nope," she said, reaching up a hand to touch the little Chihuahua. "He's so tiny."

"He is, indeed. He's got a touchy tummy, and he's been down with me for a couple days, but he's safe to bring back up."

"I can't believe I missed seeing this guy," she said, stroking the tiny head.

"He often stays behind the front desk, so you can usually find him there."

"He's gorgeous," she whispered, loving the delicate small head and the bright eyes as he stared at her. "It's quite a life he's got here, isn't it?"

"Well, it's a whole lot better than the life he would have had if he wasn't here," Stan admitted.

"How do you let them go?" she asked.

"It's hard, unless I know that they'll be in a better place," he said with a smile. "But then I'm a little bit harder to convince than a lot of people. I want to make sure every animal is safe and okay. So we end up keeping way more than we probably have to," he said, laughing, "but Dani has been great about that too."

"It seems like Dani has really forged a path for herself here."

"She has, but it was originally a path of adversity that she finally found a way forward to make her own."

"I guess that's the trick, isn't it?"

"It is, but also you are not on some deadline either," he said. "Nobody said you had to figure out everything in your life right now," he added. "And sometimes it's not that easy to figure out anyway, so it can take months to years."

"I *was* trying to figure out what I wanted to do with my life," she said. "Everything's changed now. I'm at a cross-road, where I get to make a new decision."

"Oh, I like that," Stan said. "You *get* to make new deci-sions, change directions, make new directions. Those are really positive words," he said, "You're not at a point where you *have to*, but you *get to*." He nodded. "Good way to look at it."

Even after he left, she frowned at him, considering his insights into her use of that term, and he was right; it was a good way to look at it. She hadn't realized that she had moved from "have to" onto "get to."

When Shane sat down in front of her, she beamed. "Hey, you."

He laughed and said, "Hey. How're you doing?"

"Well, I just had a fun conversation with Stan." She told Shane about it and said, "But what really got me was how he reacted to my words that I *get* to make a new decision about where I want to go in my life."

"And that's because Stan, like the rest of us, is aware of how much change and turmoil, chaos even, is in everybody's life here. You're all here for a reason," he said. "So, when you get through that, we all care and are interested in seeing where you all end up, where you go, what choices you make. It's fascinating for us because we invest all for your care and then wonder about what you'll do after this."

"No, I get that," she said. "And I can see how that would be somewhat of a challenge, if you care about somebody."

"A big challenge," he said. "But, so far, I haven't found anybody I've cared about quite the same way as you."

"I'm glad to hear that," she said with a twinkle in her eye. "And I haven't figured out what I want to do from here either."

"And nobody said you had to figure it out today."

"And that's what Stan just said." She stared off in the distance. "I don't want to just do nothing. Now that I can walk, and I can feel my body strengthening, I want to have a passion. I want to have something to do that's aligned with my purpose."

"And what would that be?"

She shook her head. "Honestly, I have no clue."

"Well, give yourself permission to figure it out," he said, "and then just wait and see what comes up."

"That's what I was thinking about," she said, chuckling. "It's not always that easy, but maybe it's not always that difficult."

"It definitely isn't all that difficult," he said. "Life should be easier going forward. It'll be different, and you'll have varied things to sort through, but it won't have the same pain and worry that you've had up until now."

"And won't that be different too," she said. "For the longest time I wasn't thinking about a future because I didn't think I had much of one. Now I can see that I can do something, and now the choice is, what is it I want to do?"

"Like so many people here, you have a whole different

story now," he said, "because now you *do* get that choice, you do have an option, you do have something that you can do. So it's all about you. And what you would like to do."

"And that will take time to figure out," she said, nodding. "But at least I have the time."

"Exactly," he said. "Now you have the time, so give yourself a break, and let yourself just do what you need to do to heal. Keep your mind open, think about what you want, and let it go."

"Yeah," she said.

Just then his phone rang. He hopped up and said, "See you later," and he disappeared.

She smiled and realized that what she really wanted to do was spend time with him, as much time as she could. But she didn't want to be a burden, so what would she do? While he was busy doing his thing, what did she want to be doing that would be her thing?

Whatever she decided, even just considering her options, she was up for the challenge. At least she thought so. Today of all days, at least it felt like a future was out there for her, something was out there for her. She just had to figure out exactly what that was, and good luck with that because it didn't seem like any answers were on her horizon. She would have to wait and do some in-depth thoughtful consideration on it first. That was okay too.

SHANE WAS A little more agitated than he'd been in a long time. He attended a team meeting going over multiple cases. And, of course, Melissa's name had been brought up. And one of the doctors had mentioned Shane's relationship with

Melissa. Everybody else had slowly acknowledged that they knew about it.

Only one of the other therapists had brought it up further. "Are you sure," she said to Shane, "that you are not affecting her ability to improve?"

He immediately shook his head and said, "No, I think her improvements are right on target."

"Sure, and how much of it is she doing for you versus for herself?"

"I can't answer that," he said quietly, not liking the turn of the conversation. It was to be expected in many ways, but that didn't mean he had to like it.

The other therapists stayed quiet, but then she asked, "Have you thought about backing off a little bit, just to see if it does affect how she does?"

"It would be hard to explain to her," he said, "why all of a sudden I'm not having anything to do with her, and I think that, in itself, would cause confusion and hurt instead of her own backward progress. And that's not what we want." He kept his voice calm and contained, but it was not an unusual conversation, given the circumstances. He'd attended many when it was based on other people than himself. He just didn't like having the spotlight turned on him. Nobody did.

One of the doctors said, "Well, you could try it for a day or two, and just see if there's any change."

"Not a day or two," he said. "It'll just confuse her."

The doctor nodded slowly. "Well, maybe just ease things back a little bit, make it not quite so dominant in your world."

"Is it wrong to want to spend time with a patient?" he asked. "We've seen it time and time again here."

"It's absolutely not wrong," Dani said quietly at his side.

He gave her a grateful smile, appreciating her endorsement, her championship. But her next words brought home to him just how many problems could be here.

"The thing is, if anybody has any issues over this, it's always been our policy to keep an open thought process moving on it."

"So what am I to do?" he asked. "I don't really want to set her back."

"No, of course not," Dani said. "Maybe I'll talk to her," she said thoughtfully. "I do know her better than anybody else here."

"Are you sure that's wise?" Shane asked.

The doctor spoke up. "That seems like we're just getting things more confused."

"I don't think so," Dani said. "I think there's room for a lot more clarity here than we're giving Melissa allowances for."

"Do you really think that she doesn't see him as some kind of a savior?" the doctor continued.

"I would hope not," Shane said. "I'm very much a simple man with the same lead feet as all of us." He kept his voice cool, making sure not to point any fingers or to bring up any names, because everybody here had had multiple reasons to question their own abilities. There was always a hard case, always somebody who didn't respond, always somebody who had an attitude issue that grated a nerve or two. He knew he wasn't alone, worrying about the progress of a patient.

"And now that we've decided that Dani will speak with Melissa," he said, somewhat forcibly, "let's move on to the next case. I am quite concerned about Nash, who's arriving next week. I think it's a little early, considering his surgery was only last week."

"I wondered about that too," Dani said quietly. "His doctor has okayed it though."

"But then how much of that is because they're short on space?"

"That's always a problem we're up against, isn't it?" she said with a heavy sigh. "I'll contact the doctor again to make sure it's still a go."

"We do have a good medical staff here too," the doctor said. "If traveling here so soon after his surgery is a problem, it just means his progress will be slower as we get him stabilized."

"And that's really not what our role here is," she muttered. "But it seems like, in some cases, some of the treating doctors are just fobbing their patients off early, putting them in our hands."

"And sometimes I think it's for the best too," Shane said with a wry tone. "Here, at least, we can work with them on a one-to-one basis, and they can progress at a much faster rate than they would if they were still back where they aren't wanted."

"It's always a fine balance, isn't it? We can't bring in everybody because we just don't have space or the facilities or the staff to handle it," Dani said. "But maybe it's time I had a little bit deeper conversation with him."

"Has Nash been told he's coming?"

"Yes," she said with a nod. "I haven't spoken to him directly though. I'll add that to my list today."

After that, they moved into a series of different conversations, and, by the time Shane walked out, he felt better than if he'd walked out earlier.

Dani caught him as they were leaving. "May I speak with you for a few minutes?"

He nodded and headed to her office. He didn't know exactly what the conversation would entail, but always something was going on in Dani's world. He sat down in the visitor's chair and said, "Thank you for stepping in to talk to Melissa."

"And I need to talk to you. Melissa's had a pretty rough go-around in many ways," she said. "So, as a friend, I also don't want her hurt."

He looked at Dani, frowned, then nodded. "Right. You're caught in between, aren't you?"

"She is a friend of mine. She came here at my persuasion," she said. "I figured we could do an awful lot for her, and I've been proven right. You're a fantastic therapist."

"But," he said, waiting for the pin to drop.

She smiled. "The only thing I want to say is that I just want to make sure that she's not hurt in all this either. Some hurt comes along with life, and we can't protect everybody from everything. But I do need to know how you feel about her."

"All I can tell you at this point is," he said, "I'll be devastated when she leaves."

She sighed and sat back. "I guess that's partly why I'm asking. Are you leaving with her?"

She surprised him once more, and his instinctive reaction was to shout *no* across the room. But, of course, she was concerned. He was the head of the physiotherapy department, and replacing him—while he didn't have a large-enough ego to think it would be difficult—it would be trying, and training would be involved. He shook his head and said, "No, I'm not planning on leaving at all." He watched the relief whisper across her face.

"You know all this stuff really does bring up emotions and problems for everybody else, doesn't it?"

He stared off in the distance and said, "I didn't even think about it. I didn't try to go in this direction."

"Good," she said. "That sounds wrong to think of somebody even attempting to do that. It's always better when it happens naturally. At one point in time, I suspect you do want to move on," she said. "I can't force you to stay. I can't persuade you to stay, but it's good to know that you're not looking to leave."

"No, I'm not. Do you know if she has any plans?" he asked her.

"I think she's still figuring out her options. I know she's always had a love of animals, but I don't know if she's up for going back to school or not. I don't know how her body would handle that yet either."

"I'm not exactly sure," he said. "Obviously we can get her to the point where she can go. Whether it's a viable option, considering how tiring it might be for her, I don't know."

Dani nodded. "It's one of the things that I want to talk to her about."

"I'm hoping you don't discuss our relationship," he said carefully.

She smiled at him. "I'll bring up what I need to," she said. "I just need to know where her thoughts are about you, so I know if we're dealing with something that's professional or personal."

"Dear God," he said. "I would really hate for her feelings toward me to be solely based on anything other than deep and profound personal reasons."

"And that's partly why I want to talk to her because you're special to us too. I don't want you hurt. I don't want her hurt. I'd like to head off something before it becomes a problem. But I can see that it's already something that should have been brought up before."

"I don't think so," he said. "We weren't really there. In truth, I don't know where we are."

She laughed out loud. "And that's perfect," she said warmly. "Nobody should really know where they are at this point. Life is for living, so stop trying to plan it. Just get out there and enjoy it."

And, on that note, he got up with a silly grin on his face, walked out, and, of course, he headed for Melissa's room, just to check in and to say hi because something about seeing that smile of hers made every day all that much brighter.

Chapter 11

MELISSA LOOKED UP several days later to see Dani walking into her room. "Hey," she said, taking a good look at her friend. "Don't you look tired?" Melissa noted, her tone of voice serious.

"Tired, yes," Dani said. "I've been pondering for a couple days how to broach a subject, wishing I could assign it to someone else."

"Okay," Melissa said, straightening up slowly. "This sounds serious."

Dani gave her a crooked smile and said, "Well, that depends. The question really is, how serious are things between you and Shane?"

Immediately Melissa gasped and said, "Oh, my gosh. Is it becoming a problem for him? I just wanted to be ... friendly."

"The thing is, are you being more than friendly just trying to be friendly? How serious is it in your heart?" she asked. "Because I'm in an odd position. Not only are you my friend but Shane's my friend. I don't want to see either of you hurt."

"And yet, as you well know," Melissa said, "you can't protect me from every ill in the world, and you can't save me from all the hurts in the world."

"I know," Dani said sadly. "I wish I had that crystal ball

that would tell me how you could avoid it all, but I don't."

She laughed with a joyous peal of laughter. "No, you sure don't," she said, "but that's okay. Neither do I. It's not like that's a mandatory thing as far as Shane and I are concerned," she said. "I really like him. He's a sweetheart."

"As in somebody you want to stay in touch with when you leave here?"

Melissa stared at her in shock. "Are you asking if my intentions are good?"

Dani shot her a cheeky grin. "Yeah, in some ways I am." She walked over and sat on the bed beside her. "You and I have been friends for a long time, and Shane and I have been friends for a long time. There's a certain amount of strife just because he's here and you're a patient, so it's up to me to make sure that everybody is happy, healthy, and willing in this joint venture of yours."

"Absolutely," she said. "He's a wonderful guy. I'm not sure how I was ever so lucky to have caught his interest, but I really don't want to mess up anything and lose it. You know what my relationship history is like."

"I do," she said, "and I know that, from your perspective, it really sucks, but I don't think it's quite as bad as you think it to be."

"I think it's that bad," she said. "And Shane's a really nice guy. I really care about him."

"So, as in a *permanent forever-after* type of care, or as in *Hey, we'll take it on a fun road trip and see where we go?*"

"You know what?" she said. "I try not to make any plans, and I've never really been very good at going after what I want or telling people when to stop because I can't do it anymore, so you're bringing up some personal issues."

"Good," Dani said. "That's all important too."

"*Argh,*" Melissa said. "I just assumed it wasn't. I hope you're not having the same conversation with Shane."

"No. It was brought up in a team meeting a few days ago as to whether the relationship is impacting your ability to improve or not."

"I can't see that it has been," she said. "I can see that maybe people would get the wrong impression about how I feel about him, and that's not what I would want him to worry about. Obviously a lot of very grateful patients have been in his life, and obviously ..." She stopped, confused. She took a deep breath and said, "Obviously I'm grateful. That goes without saying. He's helped me a lot, and I can see a ton of progress, but I can also see where everybody else is a little worried that my emotions are a bit caught up between thankfulness and actual caring."

"Maybe other people," Dani said gently, "but not me. I know you."

She smiled at her friend. "Well, you do and you don't. You haven't known me for a while. I don't want Shane to pay a price that I wasn't really counting had to be paid."

"It doesn't," Dani said, cheerfully hopping up. "And it particularly doesn't if I know that you care about him as a person."

"Well, that's a definite yes," she said with a smile.

"Good," she said. "Then we'll leave it that you guys can work your way through this."

"Is it always this hard?" she asked.

"Well, I didn't have a great set of relationships in my history either," she said. "What I have with Aaron is 100 percent different than anything I had ever thought was possible. So maybe take all those expectations and previous history of your past relationships and throw them out the window and just work toward allowing something brand new to come in. I think you'll be pleasantly surprised at what you can create out of this."

"And should I be trying to create something or just letting something develop naturally?" she asked. "I've spent a lot of time thinking about this. I don't want to push him. I don't want him to feel like, you know, I'm on his case every day or even there all the time. I don't want to do anything to chase him away either."

"And, of course, you're worried about that need to belong again," Dani said. "And I do understand that."

"I'm glad you do," she said with a half smile, "because I'm not sure I do. It could dominate so much in my life right now."

"Again, maybe decide what you want. Go after it, and then, once you've stated your intentions, let things fall into place and see how it develops. It's all about trust and communication. With those two things you can do so much more in life." She reached over, gave Melissa a big hug. "I'm so grateful that you came here."

"You're grateful?" Melissa said with a big laugh. "I'm the one who's grateful. I was stuck, and I couldn't see what you were trying to tell me as even being a possibility, but now that I'm here—Wow! It's just so incredible. I want to pay it back by doing something to help someone, something in the world too, and I feel like sometimes I'm just so frustrated because I don't know where to go from here."

"And again, that's because you didn't think that *here*, where you are right now, was even a possibility, so trying to figure it out, how to go from here, is a whole new concept."

"It seems like everybody's telling me that lately," she said.

Dani gave a laugh, lifted her hand in a wave, and walked out the door.

As she left, Melissa realized just how much of a friend Dani was. Melissa was not only here because Dani was concerned about Melissa but also about her friend Shane.

At that time, Shane walked in the door to her room, just missing Dani. He looked at Melissa, smiled, and said, "Hey, gorgeous."

She laughed. "Now, you see? If I actually was gorgeous," she said, "I'd think you meant that. The fact that I'm only just now recovering from walking like a crab, going sideways …"

"And that's because, once again, you're stuck thinking on the outside, not the inside," he said. "Remember? Here we don't worry so much about the outside because we know how much it can change. Here we're all about the inside. And honestly, your inside is beautiful. It's a little insecure, a little shaky. But it's come so far."

"I heard you got asked about our relationship and questioned about whether it was helping me or hurting me." She said it so abruptly that the smile fell away from his face.

He nodded slowly. "Yes, and that's standard procedure. We've had a lot of relationships come together here," he said, "and it's always about the patient, what's good for them, what they need, versus what's good for me or anybody else."

"That doesn't sound very fair," she said.

"We're not the ones who are recovering from major trauma, with massive life changes. The meeting was just fine. Don't you worry about it."

She sat back, happy with his answer. "So you're not …" She didn't know quite what to say.

He looked up at her. "I'm not what?"

"You're not regretting being friends with me?"

His eyebrows shot up. "No," he said. "It's what *I* want, so it won't matter who says what." And just then his phone rang. He pulled it from his pocket and looked at it. "I'm late for another meeting. I have to run." He took off in a jog.

She worried about his words for a long time afterward. She sat here on her bed until it was lunchtime, and then she managed to walk slowly and carefully down the hallway. She was so much better obviously but still months away from doing this without collapsing and exhausting herself. However, her progress was obvious—more than obvious, it was incredible.

As she stepped in line and picked up a tray, still mindful of her actions, Dennis walked over with a big smile and said, "What can I get for you today?"

"How about some self-confidence?" she said, as if she were reading a grocery list. "A dose of forward-thinking and some idea of what I was put on this planet to do."

He stared at her with surprise; then a huge grin flashed across his face. "Done," he said. "Absolutely. No problem with that."

She stared at him with as much surprise as he'd had, while he dished her up a great big salad with a grilled chicken breast off to the side, some steamed vegetable medley that looked delicious next to it. She said, "This doesn't look like what I ordered."

"Well, like all things in life on a big level, you said it takes a bit of time. All you really have to do to get the answers to all of what you just asked for," he said, "is go inside and trust. Check out your heart. You'll find all the answers you need are right there. It's usually insecurity and fear that stops us from going after what we really want. After that, it's all just noise. Stop listening to the noise. Find the goodness inside, and you'll get all the answers you want. See? It's easy." And he turned to the guy behind her and asked, "What can I get you today?"

And, with that, she had to be satisfied. She picked up her tray and slowly walked to a table. As she sat down, her mind was turning over Dennis's words. Because such a kernel of truth was in there, a kernel of honesty and decency, and, yes, realization that what she was really doing was looking outside herself for the answers, when all she had to do was look inside.

SHANE HAD TO admit that, as much as he didn't like it, he felt like he walked a little bit more carefully around Melissa for the next few days.

Finally on Friday, she headed to his office, faced him, and said, "Spit it out."

He looked at her, questioning. "Spit what out?"

"Whatever is bugging you," she said.

And just enough exasperation and frustration were in her voice that he had to chuckle. "And what if nothing's bugging me?"

"Well, obviously something is," she said. "And I don't know what it is, but I would like to know. And, if it's more of that craziness that got you into trouble at the meeting or that I had to talk with Dani about, we need to put a stop to it right now."

He turned toward her. "What would you like to do with that?"

"Go forward," she said instantly.

"In what direction?" he asked cautiously, studying her.

She looked almost spitting mad but not quite, as if she were just a step or two away from losing it, and that was something he had yet to see.

"I'd like to see where this can go," she said. "In all honesty, I feel like you've been pulling back from me."

"I don't think I've been pulling back as much as I'm making sure you have space."

"Did I ask for space?" she demanded.

"No, you didn't," he admitted. "But you also don't ask when you need help or speak up when it's too far gone or when something needs to stop." He watched her wince at that. "So I'm just giving you a chance, without trying to upset you, to give you a bit of distance."

"Well, I don't like it," she snapped.

He nodded. "Can't say I like it either."

"Then stop it," she ordered. "Immediately."

He faced her, then started to laugh and laugh.

She stood here with her hands on her hips and said, "Why? What's so funny?"

"You," he said, "because, honestly, when you make up your mind about something, you're quite adamant. But, until you make up your mind, you're insecure about it."

"I think everybody is," she said.

"And I agree with that," he said. "I think most people are insecure, until they make up their mind, and then they're right there. I just hadn't really seen it blossom before in you."

Color washed up her cheeks at his words.

He smiled gently and said, "And I like it."

Somebody called out from the doorway. He turned to see his next patient.

"And you, my dear, need to head back to whatever you're up to next."

She groaned. "I think it's more lab tests."

"Good," he said. "I'll be interested to see how they turn out."

"Meaning that my nutrition might be getting better?"

"I think that all the supplementations—and those lovely green drinks that I know you don't like—should be helping. This will give us a marker to let us know for sure."

She nodded agreeably and, moving carefully but upright, she headed for the door.

As she got there, he whistled and said, "By the way, it's looking really good."

She tossed him a cheeky smile and said, "So are you," and disappeared around the corner.

He was still smiling to himself as Arnold walked in. "Well, I don't know what medicine you're giving her," he said, "but I want some too."

At that, Shane burst out laughing. "Same medicine as everybody else," he said. "Just lots of hard work."

"Oh, I don't know. Something pretty special seems to be going on between you two."

"I hope so," Shane said. "It'd be nice if I would get that lucky."

"Ah, so now we're talking about lucky," Arnold said, a twinkle in his eyes.

Shane shook his head. "I've watched a lot of relationships form in this place over the last year," he said with a smile. "I just didn't think it would ever happen to me."

"It's always hard being on the outside, isn't it? Everybody else doesn't always realize just what it's like to watch all those around you have a stroke of good luck, and you're sitting here wondering when and how your world will ever get a break. And then, *boom!* Just like that, it's changed."

"Something like that, yes," he said. "And I really didn't think it would change anytime soon for me. But surprise, surprise."

"I like her. She's nice," Arnold said.

"Have you had much to do with her?" Shane asked, curious.

"No, but she's always around. She's always polite and friendly. She's always got a smile, you know? And I don't care how beautiful a woman is or how much a woman does to make herself beautiful, but, when a natural smile comes from her heart, … it's more beautiful than anything they could ever do to their face."

"I agree with you there. I don't think she really sees that inner beauty."

"And that just adds to it," he said. "You're not always dealing with her ego then."

"And yet there's often an insecurity issue," he reminded Arnold.

"And that just means that she's insecure about where she stands. Make her feel better about that, and you'll see her really blossom."

Arnold's words stayed with Shane for a long time. He knew, in theory, that was quite true. He'd seen it time and time again with self-confidence in other patients. And he wasn't sure just what the core issue was with Melissa, but he wanted to be there to see that same blossoming in her. And he wanted it to happen because of him and because she wanted to be with him.

"Which isn't asking for much," he muttered to himself. And truly maybe it wasn't, but it was something that mattered. And that meant he had to do something about it.

Chapter 12

MELISSA HAD MEANT what she had said to Shane, to Dani, but still that weird disconnect continued on around her. She didn't like it one bit. Finally a few days later, she debated whether she should even go into the dining room for lunch. She felt ... out of sorts. Then she realized she needed food because it's the only way she would build up enough strength to move herself out of here.

Just the thought of leaving Shane dropped pain into her heart. As she walked with her tray, she frowned at the food.

"Uh-oh," Dennis said, "I don't like the look on that face."

She looked up in surprise, then shrugged. "I was just thinking about taking something and going outside with it," she said. "I'm feeling a little bit closed in."

"In that case," he said, "if you're up for some sandwiches or some hot pot pies, I'll make up a picnic basket that you could take outside."

"Oh." She tilted her head at him. "Is that possible?"

"In my kitchen, anything's possible," he said.

She smiled. "I'd really like that. I'd like to spend some time with the animals."

"Be right back then," he said. He disappeared into the kitchen, even with other people in line behind her.

She looked around a little worriedly, but another woman

came from the kitchen and took his place, proceeding to help everybody else in the line. Melissa stepped aside. As long as she wasn't holding people up, it was all good.

Dennis came back a few minutes later and walked around the buffet, so he was out of the kitchen area, then gave her a wicker basket. He said, "Try this for size."

She lifted it and said, "It's not too bad for weight, but it feels like a lot of food." She frowned at it. "I didn't need much. Just a sandwich would be good."

"Nope, not around here," he said. "We do picnics all the time. Go and enjoy."

She nodded, said thank you, and, as she began to walk away, he called out, "Are you okay otherwise?"

She looked back at him, smiled, and said, "Yeah. Just lots to think about, you know? Like you said, go inside and find some answers. But it's hard to find time and space to go inside."

He nodded with understanding. "That's the truth. Don't be surprised if somebody finds you out there and comes to join you."

"That's fine," she said. "I'm not trying to be alone. I'm just trying to get out of the space I'm in."

And, with that, she turned and slowly, carefully walked to the elevator. She was still not as confident in her footsteps as she would like to be at this point in time of her recovery. The fact that she was doing as well as she had was a testament to Dani's team. And then Melissa had to trust and follow through, and that was the testament to herself. She had to remember to give herself kudos for following and believing and putting her faith in these people, who had it all worked out for her, which was just a huge boon. Now she had to figure out what to do after this. And Shane was a big part of that.

Taking the stairs outside the clinic, she slowly moved toward the pathway, wondering if she would have been smarter to have brought the wheelchair; this would be one of the longest walks she'd ever done—not that she was against it, but she didn't want to tire herself out.

Stan was outside with several dogs, walking them around.

"I didn't think about it," she said, as she called out to Stan, "but I guess they all need to get out and to get exercise and to have bathroom breaks too, don't they?"

"They do, and I need fresh air and exercise too." He motioned at the picnic basket. "Where are you going?"

"Down the pathway to where the horses are. The walls were starting to close in on me."

He nodded in understanding. "Helga would love to go with you, if you want company," he said. "But no pressure if you just want to be alone."

She looked at him, as a great big Newfoundlander was already halfway toward her. "Will she stay with me?"

"We're fully fenced out here, so she can't go far," he said. "And you can bet that she would love to go anywhere with you. She loves being outside, and she adores the horses."

"Well, if I am not in any danger of having to chase after her or losing her," she said, "then I'd love to have the company."

"Good." He called Helga over, and she came running. He gave her a good scratch behind the ears and said, "Would you prefer to have a leash on her?"

"No. I'm not that stable on my feet," she said instantly. "As long as she's okay to be free and running all by herself.

But maybe I shouldn't …"

"She's perfect," he said. "Just keep walking and call her to you. She'd love to come."

And, with that, Melissa headed out, smiling to see Helga immediately coming after her. "She really does like to be out with us, doesn't she?"

"With anybody and everybody, and she doesn't even know she hasn't got but three legs," he said.

"Which makes it perfect for her," she said with a bright smile. "That's what we all need to do. Just realize life happens, deal with it, and move on."

Stan nodded and asked, "Are you okay then?"

She flashed him a bright smile. "I am, indeed," she said. "Just one of those days, you know, where you wake up out of sorts, and you're not sure why."

"Oh, yeah," he said. "Especially in a place like this. Lots happening on all different levels." He lifted his hands, then called the other dogs back with him.

She kept walking, loving the fresh air and sunshine with a bit of a breeze. It was just enough to lift the tendrils of hair from the back of her neck, cooling her off a bit. She should probably go down to the swimming pool eventually and really cool down, something she hadn't done yet. She'd been in the hot tub but hadn't really done any water lessons with Shane. There'd been a lot to work on, and she'd never asked.

Just one of the things that Shane had recently mentioned, about speaking up for herself. If she wanted something, she needed to say so, and, if she didn't want to do something, she needed to say so. She'd gone along with that tribe mentality for a long time. The navy was like that. They went in groups, large groups. They followed orders; your day was a block of time, and it was all laid out for you.

Now here she was, with more time on her hands than she'd ever had in her life, and she was a little bit at loose ends, not sure what to do. Not that it had to stay that way, but it made her wonder just what she should be doing.

Finally she came to a spot that had a little bit of a rise in a bit of a flat spot, so she got off the path very carefully, took several steps down onto the grass, and sat down, careful of her picnic basket. She still didn't know what was in it, and curiosity was killing her because Dennis was such a great guy at producing food, even though she knew a full kitchen team was in the background. But, if anybody could pull off something to put a smile on her face, she was pretty sure it was him.

She opened the basket to find a little tablecloth. With a chuckle she spread it out, even as Helga immediately laid down on top of it. "I don't think that's what it's meant for," she said, reaching out to scratch Helga on the back of the neck.

Helga just gave her a light *woof* and rolled over, exposing her belly. Melissa accommodated her, giving her a nice rub on her belly. When Helga seemed satisfied, Melissa chuckled and went back into the basket to find more items wrapped up there, things not easily identified. She pulled out the one on the top and realized it was a small pot pie. It looked like a chicken pot pie, and it smelled delicious, and it was still warm.

Her stomach immediately started growling, and, whereas she hadn't been hungry before, now she was ravenous. Her appetite was taking advantage of being outside with the fresh air. She kept pulling out more and more items. Realizing that she couldn't eat half of this, she shook her head and said out loud, "What on earth were you thinking?"

"Knowing Dennis," a man said, "he was thinking that you probably wouldn't be alone."

She looked up to see Shane walking toward her, a broad smile on his face. She laughed with delight when he asked, "May I join you?"

Helga gave a soft *woof* and thumped her tail, but she didn't stray from her spot on the tablecloth covering the ground.

Melissa chuckled. "Helga says, yes. Please," she said. "I just needed to get outside for a little bit. The walls were closing in on me. Everybody's telling me to figure stuff out, but I'm not getting any answers, so feeling a little bit like a failure ..." she admitted.

"Ah," he said, "we all have down days." He sat down near Helga, giving her a gentle ear rub.

"And I know I shouldn't let these down days get to me," she said, "but that doesn't seem to stop them from showing up, even though I tell them to stay away."

"None of us have all the answers," he said. "All we can do is give you suggestions. The answers are inside you, and it doesn't matter what we say. It's all got to be your way."

"I get that," she said. "It's just a little frustrating when the answers aren't coming."

"Understood. We've all been there." He looked at the basket and the contents she'd spread out and said, "Wow. Dennis really did fill you up, didn't he?"

"He's deadly," she said. "A lot of food here."

"Not that that's a problem," Shane said, "*if* you're shar-ing."

Helga let out another *woof.*

They both chuckled, as they shook their heads at the completely relaxed dog in their midst.

"I'm surprised she's not interested in our food," Shane noted.

"Looking at her," Melissa said, "I would say she gets plenty of feedings during the day."

Shane nodded. "I suspect all the animals are spoiled here, if Dani has anything to do with it."

Melissa laughed, and they each reached for a separate pot pie. "It looks like there's definitely two of everything," she frowned. "Did he tell you that I was out here?"

"Nope. But I was in the lunchroom, looking for you, wondering if you were going to eat or how your day was going," he said. "I didn't have a session with you today, so I didn't get my daily top-up."

"I know," she said. "It's funny just how much I miss our connection on a day that we don't have something together."

"Well, we don't have to rely on scheduled sessions though," he said. "We can have lunches together, coffee together, dinner together."

She smiled. "That almost sounds like a date."

"It absolutely sounds like a date," he said. "The question is whether that's something you're interested in or not?"

She looked at him, smiled, and said, "Absolutely. I wasn't kidding when I said that I really wanted to figure all this out. That I didn't want to lose track of you."

"Not losing track of me," he said, "leaves an awful lot open to interpretation."

She frowned as she thought about that and then nodded. "I want to continue getting to know you," she said. "It feels like I know you, but I don't know as much as I would like to."

"And how do you get to really know somebody?" he asked curiously.

"Spend a lot of time with them."

"Or seeing them in tough times," he said with a gentle grin. "That can shorten that time frame really fast."

"Back to that's why the relationships here flourish on a very different level, isn't it?"

"Absolutely. Just think of a real soul-deep relationship and how many layers are involved, and then think about how different a social more superficial relationship is and how long it takes to get through all those layers."

She nodded in understanding. "Who knows how many layers because of the surgeries and just not dealing with that superficial level anymore."

"Exactly," he said. "So I ask you again. How do you feel about it being a date?"

She smiled, took a deep breath, and shyly said, "I'd love it."

"Perfect," he said. "So now that we've got that settled, what else is bothering you?"

"It's not so much bothering me," she said, "as much as I'm still feeling rootless, directionless."

"And why is that?"

She winced.

He caught the look that crossed her face and said, "You know that you can tell me anything, right?"

"I know," she said, "and it goes back to needing to tell you something important, needing to tell you what's happening, when I'm ready to stop or when I'm ready to start something or if I want something and haven't asked for it. It's all wrapped up in itself."

"So that sounds a bit ominous. I'm glad we got the date part through first."

She laughed. "Well, we did, but it's connected."

He stared at her, one eyebrow raised, waiting.

But she wasn't quite ready. She shrugged and said, "It's not that easy."

"None of this is," he said. He finished his pie, rooted around inside the basket, and said, "What else have we got here?"

"You tell me," she said, digging in beside him. "It looks like a lot, but I'm not exactly sure."

He smiled. "Looks like we have a bunch here." He pulled out small bowls with tops on them. "Salads," he immediately handed her one and kept himself one, pulling out two forks from the bottom of the basket.

"I can tell you one thing I'd like to do though," she said, "and I'm not used to asking for stuff, so this isn't an easy one."

"If you're not used to doing it, nothing's easy," he said. "So what are you asking for?"

"Can I get in the pool?"

She said it in such a sad contemplative tone that he burst out laughing. "Absolutely you can get in the pool," he said. "It was on my notes to ask you last week, and I completely forgot about it."

"Yeah, it's been a little busy around here, hasn't it?"

"It's been busy, but it's been great because you've moved ahead so fast."

"Do you think that I'm slowing down now?"

"Maybe this last week, yeah. I wasn't sure if there was a reason for it or not."

"Well, there's a reason, but it goes back to that ... I'm not really sure how I should be dealing with some of this."

"Okay, that sounds ominous again."

"Maybe I'm just not sure that I'm ready."

"Then no pressure," he said, surprising her.

She smiled at him. "You know something? You're a really nice man."

He stopped and stared at her. "Somehow that doesn't sound terribly complimentary."

"Well, it's meant to be," she said.

"So are you, a nice woman, that is."

They sat, eating in comfortable silence. She wondered just how much she could tell him, and she wasn't sure that she even knew all the answers.

But her progress had definitely slowed down, and she'd noticed it. Everybody kept talking about her progress up until now, and she figured that that was part of what put her mood off. Some kernel remained in the back of her mind as to what might be going on in the background, but she didn't really have any way to work through it.

SHANE STUDIED MELISSA'S face, as he tried to enjoy his salad. He had noticed her lack of progress this last week, almost ten days now, but he wondered if she had. He hadn't brought it to her attention because it was often a mistake to point out the negative things. But something was going on. "Are you upset about your lack of progress?"

"Well, I guess plateaus happen," she said with a shrug. "Like any weight loss, you lose a bit, and then you plateau. But you carry on."

He laughed at the analogy, but it was fairly accurate. "That's true enough," he said. "I don't really have any rhyme or reason at the moment for why there's a slowdown overall on the progress, particularly after we made progress with your walking. So it could be a combination of things."

She nodded thoughtfully, staring at the horses.

He could sense almost as if she'd pulled an invisible cloak around her, keeping her thoughts to herself. "And this is one of the reasons why," he said, "you need to open up to let other people in."

"Do you think it's me?" She looked at him suddenly.

"I don't know," he said, staring back steadily. "It's possible. It happens, and it can happen for all different kinds of reasons."

"I don't want it to be me because that means I don't want to get better," she said, the words rushing out of her.

"I don't think that's the reason at all," he said, understanding a little of what was happening. "Any number of things from your past could be running around in your head, even right now, that's slowing you down or making you doubt yourself or causing all kinds of things that would slow your progress. And it could be just that your body needs time to catch up."

"I like that last one," she said with relief.

He smiled at her, then dug back into the basket. "So we have giant cookies, and a thermos is in here."

"You think that's coffee?" she asked in delight.

He opened it up, sniffed, and said, "Absolutely it's coffee." He smiled at two cups but said with a frown, "There's no cream."

"And no sugar?" she asked. "I don't take either."

"Neither do I," he said. He opened the thermos and poured both of them a cup.

They sat here, sipping their coffee, and she asked, "So the cookies are our dessert?"

"You take a look," he said. "I'll lie down and close my

eyes." And he put his coffee cup beside him, stretched out on the grass because Helga still had the entire tablecloth. When she realized Shane was lying down, her tail thumped him hard, whacking him in the arm, but she then continued to snooze right beside him.

He just lay here, watching the clouds above float, letting his whole body ease back. It was so nice to be here in Mother Nature with Melissa—and Helga and the other animals. He knew in his mind he worried about Melissa's lack of progress, but, at the same time, his heart was happy about it, as it meant she would be here longer. The faster she recovered meant the better for her, but, if it took her away from him earlier, before they had a chance to really figure out where they were at, that wouldn't make him happy.

The silence hung in the air for a long time, and he wondered if he would be allowed to just snooze here, when she said suddenly, "I think I'm doing it to myself."

"Interesting," he said. "And why do you think that?"

"I'm not sure. Something in the back of my head tells me that it's me. That I'm holding myself back." She looked at him. "Who does that?"

"Everybody does that," he said. Immediately he rolled over and propped himself up on an elbow. "That's what you have to realize. Everybody does it."

She looked at him with a serious gaze. "Are you just saying that to make me feel better?"

He chuckled. "I have better things to do than that. I deal with lots of patients every day. I've seen hundreds since I've begun working here, probably thousands," he said. "Almost everybody has a crisis of faith in themselves, in the world around them, in their own spiritual path, in a relationship. But particularly in the relationship they have with themselves."

She stared at him and then turned toward the pastures. "You see? If I were a horse," she said, looking at the horses in front of them, "I could just eat, sleep, and the biggest problem I would have to work out is which blade of grass to pick up and eat."

"And, if you were a horse," Shane said immediately, "you would have your face to the sun, and you would enjoy the peace and quiet. You would be living in today, whether you had an injury or not. You wouldn't be worrying about how other horses would see you. You wouldn't be worrying about past horses you might have known, and neither would you be worrying about future horses that you have yet to find."

She started to laugh and laugh and laugh.

He grinned at her.

"Oh, that's good," she said. "That's really good."

"And it's true," he said. "Remember. Stop pushing yourself so hard to find answers. What do you want right now?" he asked.

She rolled over so she could look at him and said, "Peace of mind."

"That sounds good to me, and what is it that's stopping you from achieving peace of mind?"

"Trying to figure out why I have stopped progressing."

"And you can't just let it be and realize that it's a natural state of affairs?" he asked curiously.

She grimaced at that. "It feels like a cop-out when you say that you think it's because of me, that I'm the one who slowed down my healing." She nodded. "That's how it feels."

"Okay. Go with that," he said. "What else is it that you need to do in order to change that?"

"I need to understand why I would slow my progress."

"Because you're afraid to succeed," he said instantly.

"Oh, that's a big one, isn't it?" She flopped over on her back, put her arms up above her head, and smiled at the green grass tickling her fingers. "It's so beautiful out here, and it's so odd to think that we set ourselves up for failure."

"We do it all the time," he said.

"What are you afraid of?" she asked suddenly.

He smiled and said, "Not being good enough. That, should I end up in a place like this someday, would I handle it as well as the rest of you have? And another big one is not getting something that I really, really want."

"And what's that?"

"It doesn't have to be anything specific," he said, "but whenever I really, really want something, a part of me is terrified that I won't get it. And, if I don't get it, I'll walk through life always feeling the lack of not having it."

"Are we talking commercial things? You know? Like stuff. Like a teakettle?"

He bolted upright on his elbows and stared at her, saying, "Do you think I really, really want a teakettle?"

But she had a sassy grin on her face.

He shook his head. "No, but it's like getting to be the physiotherapist that I am right now," he said. "That was a goal. It was a really big goal, and it worried away at me for a long time—even when I graduated, and I had that piece of paper—that I wasn't a physiotherapist until I had a job, working in this field."

"Ah," she said. "So achieving things."

"Yes. But it's not just about achieving things," he said, "because there's more to life than that."

"I guess," she said. "I can't think of anything that I really, really wanted and couldn't have."

"Maybe you're not the person who dares to care," he said.

She rolled her head over to look at him. "No," she said. "I think I care so much but know I can't have what I want, so I already sabotaged my ability to have it. So, knowing I can't have it, therefore, I don't want it."

He stared at her, then worked his way through the convoluted explanation. "Ah, so you refuse to think about it before you start? You won't allow yourself to want because you already know you can't have it?"

"Exactly."

Chapter 13

M ELISSA KNEW IT was foolish, but that's how she felt. He picked a blade of grass and separated the leaf from it. She watched those very capable fingers as he worked away, his gaze obviously dropped down to study the grass. Yet she didn't think he saw the grass but something else in his head. "What?"

He looked up and smiled. "I think it's just a lack of security again," he said, "because you're so afraid you can't have something, and there is bound to be a part of you that feels you'll lose it anyway."

"And that takes me back to my family, yes," she said. "You don't realize what losing your entire family as a teenager can do to you."

"And yet, when will you walk away from it, recognizing that it'll always be there," he said calmly, "but not prepared to give it the power to ruin your future?"

She stared at him for a moment. "Well, I hadn't thought of it that way. I don't want it to be always determining my future."

"However, if you hang on to that as your past," he said, "it has to be something that determines your future because there's no way it can't. It is a part of you."

"I know," she said, as she was just realizing how much she let that part of her have control over her future. "You're right. I don't want it to have that much power, and I don't want it to dominate my life, stopping me from getting something else I want."

"Good," he said. "Just understand that sometimes it's likely to come up, and you'll just recognize it and let it go. You don't have to let it be that dominant in your world anymore."

A bubble burst. Immediately such a sense of calmness and a sense of rightness filled her inside that she stared up at the blue sky and took several long, slow, deep breaths. She didn't know how to describe it to him, but it was a sense of release, letting go, like an inner tension slowly dissipating, something that she'd hung on to for a long time that she suddenly put down on the ground beside her. Then as she slowly straightened up, she could feel everything so weightless, so fresh, and just so free. She stared at the sky and wondered.

She looked at him and said, "I don't even know if I can describe what just happened." And she tried to explain.

He reached across and gripped her fingers. "I understand," he said. "It's awesome."

She smiled and felt tears in the corner of her eyes. "And why now tears?" she said, half laughing, half crying.

"It's a release," he said. "And not just women cry." He gave her a gentle smile. "Women are often teased for crying, but men cry too."

"Well, I'll be crying for a minute here," she said, as she brushed her eyes several times, as this massive wave of emotions ruptured and sent difficult feelings aside. But, at the same time, she could see the emotions as they dissipated from her system, almost with a thankfulness.

"As you see this," he said, "remember to thank it for being there for you. It was a defense mechanism. For a long time, you needed it. Now you don't."

She looked at him. "Was I really supposed to say *thank you* for that?"

"Yes," he said with a decisive nod. "Be grateful, and that will give you an avenue to a whole new world."

She closed her eyes, and, as the emotional waves pounded through her, she mentally whispered, *Thank you for being there. Thank you for helping me get to where I am right now. I am grateful.* It seemed strange, but, at the same time, an even bigger part of her felt refreshed and delighted with it all.

By the time she was done, she reached out, lifted a hand, and saw it was almost trembling. "Wow!" she said and reached up with her sleeve to wipe her eyes. "Dennis didn't put any napkins or tissues in there, did he?"

Just then Shane handed her several napkins to wipe her eyes with.

She blew her nose and sat here for a long moment. "I feel old and yet young at the same time."

"Good," he said. "That's called being reborn."

She turned and smiled at him, seeing him beside her once again. "And I also realized why I slowed my healing," she said. "I'm still uncomfortable telling you about it, but maybe it's because all this just happened that I'm feeling brave."

"So tell me," he said, sitting up to stare at her intently.

She gave a self-conscious smile and said, "Well, if I improve at the rate I should be improving," she said, "I would be doing so much better, so much faster, that my end date would be coming toward me very quickly."

"Ah," he said. "And you were afraid of what comes after that."

She shook her head. "No," she said softly. "That wasn't it at all. I mean, and it makes sense, that it would be because I don't have a job. I don't have a career. I don't even know what I want to do although ..." She turned her head to look back in the direction of the vet clinic. "I was wondering about talking to Stan about training to be an assistant in the vet clinic."

Shane looked at her in surprise. "That is a great idea," he said. "You could sit some of the time, stand some time, work with animals, be in a field that you would really love."

"I think it would be," she said. "I don't know what money would be available for retraining or how long the training itself would be, but I think it's something I would like to do. Maybe at least work in the reception area and give it a try first."

"I like the sound of that a lot," he said. "That's really a huge step, but that's not the reason you just discovered."

She took a slow, deep breath. "No," she said. "Because essentially, when I get to the point where I'm strong enough, and I'm leaving, heading into whatever this future of mine is, I'm leaving you behind."

SHANE FINALLY HEARD the words that he wanted to hear. He squeezed her fingers gently, tugged her slightly, and saw she was leaning forward too, coming his direction. Then he pulled her into his arms, where he just held her.

She started to cry again, this time soaking his shirt, and he just held her. This was definitely one of the moments to let her release all the tension and the stress inside. He rocked her gently back and forth, loving the time, the peace, the serenity with just the two of them.

Woof.

And Helga.

"And you still don't say anything," she whispered, hiccupping.

He waited for her sobs to ease back a bit before he said, "I was waiting for you to be able to hear me," he said with a note of humor.

She smiled, wiped at her eyes again, and said, "I feel like a baby. I never cry like this."

"So. It's good," he said. "This is the release you need."

"Maybe."

She tried to sit up, but he wouldn't let her. Now he said, "I'll respond because I've been waiting for you to say something like that for a long time."

She looked at him in wonder.

He looked down at her, smiled, and said, "Yes, I could have said something to you. But, in my position, where I was a caregiver, somebody working to get you back on your feet, I didn't want to influence your emotional levels by showing you just how much I did care. And I was also waiting for you to show me that you cared enough to find something that you wanted to ask for."

She closed her eyes, as if in understanding, and he nodded.

"Right. So just like you wanted to go in the pool," he said, "it's really nice to know that you want me, and you want me that much," he said, tapping her gently on the nose with his index finger.

"And does that mean that you like me as much as I like you?" she whispered.

He dropped a kiss on her forehead and held her close. "I

have no idea how much you like me," he said, "but I know that my heart smiles when it sees you, that my brain wakes up and thinks of you first thing in the morning. You're the last thought in my head before I go to sleep. And I'm looking for excuses all day long to come past your room to see if you're around."

She stared at him in astonishment.

He nodded and smiled, couldn't stop smiling now. "I've had to keep a lot of that inside," he said, "just because I'm in a professional environment. And we want you to heal. We want you to do the best you can do without it being tied up to an emotional attachment with one of us …"

"Oh, I love you for you," she said, "no doubt about that. I just hadn't realized it until all this was going on right now," she said. "I didn't realize I was sabotaging my own progress because I didn't want to leave you. It makes sense to me now. A lot of it makes sense now. But honestly, it's lovely to know that *A*, I could tell you, and that *B*, we're here."

"Isn't that the truth?" He kissed her on the nose and said, "Now, you still have a couple months here, and, in that couple months," he said, "we'll get you back on your feet, so you're as strong and as capable as you can be. We can look at various job options in the animal world, if that's where you'd like to go, and," he said, "we'll do the best we can to take our relationship one step further."

"And what does that mean?" she said in a cheeky voice.

He laughed and laughed. "Not that," he said. "Not until you're fully cleared."

"And that's sad," she said.

He hugged her tight and said, "It's something for us to wait for."

"Because it's all about living today." She smiled, reached

up, and caught his face gently with her hand. "And that's a lesson I'll delight in learning," she said. "One day at a time. Together."

"Every moment with us," he said, "is a gift. So let's just enjoy it, and later we'll work out all the details of our tomorrows." He leaned his head closer, and he kissed her gently and thoroughly.

When he finally lifted his head, she smiled and whispered, "I can get on that program. You're the best in your field. So, if you say this is what I need to do, I'm happy to follow your lead."

He shook his head and said, "In our personal relationship, you're not following anybody's lead. I want a partner who stands beside me and walks with me."

"Well, hopefully," she said, "you're also okay if I sometimes roll along in a wheelchair too."

He chuckled. "Absolutely. I don't have any requirements, other than you spend your time with me."

"Easily done," she whispered, and he lowered his head once again.

Epilogue

NASH COVINGTON LISTENED as the doctor explained once again why his trip to Hathaway was delayed. "But it's all been approved," he said in frustration. "Why is there even a discussion about it right now?"

"We're just making sure that you're well enough to travel," the doctor said. "So another four days, then you should be good to go." The doctor walked out, not willing to discuss the issue anymore, not willing to even explain any further.

Nash fell back onto his bed and groaned. His buddy Owen, beside him for many weeks, said, "So not the news you wanted?"

"Well, it's not bad news," he said. "It's just the same old bull again."

"I think they specialize in that," Owen said. "Here you seem pretty bound and determined to get to Hathaway. Are you sure it's Hathaway you want to go to, or just this place you want to get away from?"

"Probably both," Nash said. "But it's back in Dallas, and Dallas is where I want to be. That's family. That's friends. That's an old girlfriend, who I know won't want anything to do with me in this shape. But still, that doesn't mean that I won't be friends with her, and, right now, it feels like I have very little family and no friends in my life."

"I think that's the way of it," Owen said. "As soon as

you have an accident like this, you find out who your friends truly are."

"Well, not only is it the accident," he said, "but it's the accident and all the surgeries and time recovering. It's not a short-term support system. It's been what? Eighteen months now?"

"Mine's not been quite so bad," Owen said. "But, in your case, yeah. You've had a lot more surgeries."

"And I'm so ready to get out of this bed."

"How did you hear about Hathaway House?"

"A friend of mine," Nash said. "He's been gone quite a while already. But, last I heard from him, it was Hathaway House that made the difference. Cole was someone I could trust, and, if he says I'll do better there, I'd like to try."

"Then four days," Owen said. "Four more days. That's all you have to wait for now. And, when you get there, let me know if it's any good, will you?"

"Count on it, buddy. You can count on it." Nash closed his eyes, resting. If they thought he wasn't good enough to make that trip, he was bound and determined to spend the next four days doing what he could to build up his strength and to make sure that his arrival at Hathaway happened because it seemed like everybody else was against him, and that he wouldn't tolerate it. It was Hathaway or bust. Go big or go home.

Go to Hathaway House or never find a future for him again.

This concludes Book 13 of Hathaway House: Melissa.
Read about Nash: Hathaway House, Book 14

Hathaway House: Nash (Book #14)

***Welcome to Hathaway House. Rehab Center. Safe Haven.
Second chance at life and love.***

Nash has been struggling to get back on his feet after his last
set of surgeries. He pushed for a transfer to Hathaway House
on an old friend's recommendation and finally made it
there—after multiple frustrating delays—only to find that he
isn't ready for the strides he hopes to make in the new
facility.

To add insult to injury, on his first day at Hathaway
House, he comes face-to-face with Alicia, the only woman
he's ever loved and the last woman he'd want to see him in
his current condition.

Alicia let Nash go more than a decade ago, unwilling to
settle for a long-distance relationship with the sailor, certain
that her future would bring other dreams and other loves.
But, when her brother fell ill, all her dreams shattered. She
devoted herself to nursing him and, after his death, to
helping others.

Seeing Nash again is both pleasure and pain. The rapport between them is instant, as if the years apart had never happened. But, if they couldn't make things work back then, when life was bright and new, do the people they've become in the years since have a shot at a future together?

Find Book 14 here!

To find out more visit Dale Mayer's website.

https://geni.us/DMNashUniversal

Author's Note

Thank you for reading Melissa: Hathaway House, Book 13! If you enjoyed the book, please take a moment and leave a short review.

Dear reader,

I love to hear from readers, and you can contact me at my website: www.dalemayer.com or at my Facebook author page. To be informed of new releases and special offers, sign up for my newsletter or follow me on BookBub. And if you are interested in joining Dale Mayer's Reader Group, here is the Facebook sign up page.
http://geni.us/DaleMayerFBGroup

Cheers,
Dale Mayer

Get THREE Free Books Now!

Have you met the SEALS of Honor?

SEALs of Honor Books 1, 2, and 3. Follow the stories of brave, badass warriors who serve their country with honor and love their women to the limits of life and death.

Read Mason, Hawk, and Dane right now for FREE.

Go here and tell me where to send them!
https://dalemayer.com/masonfree/

About the Author

Dale Mayer is a *USA Today* best-selling author, best known for her SEALs military romances, her Psychic Visions series, and her Lovely Lethal Garden cozy series. Her contemporary romances are raw and full of passion and emotion (Broken But ... Mending, Hathaway House series). Her thrillers will keep you guessing (Kate Morgan, By Death series), and her romantic comedies will keep you giggling (*It's a Dog's Life*, a stand-alone novella; and the Broken Protocols series, starring Charming Marvin, the cat).

Dale honors the stories that come to her—and some of them are crazy, break all the rules and cross multiple genres!

To go with her fiction, she also writes nonfiction in many different fields, with books available on résumé writing, companion gardening, and the US mortgage system. All her books are available in print and ebook format.

Connect with Dale Mayer Online

Dale's Website – www.dalemayer.com

Twitter – @DaleMayer

Facebook Page – geni.us/DaleMayerFBFanPage

Facebook Group – geni.us/DaleMayerFBGroup

BookBub – geni.us/DaleMayerBookbub

Instagram – geni.us/DaleMayerInstagram

Goodreads – geni.us/DaleMayerGoodreads

Newsletter – geni.us/DaleNews

Also by Dale Mayer

Published Adult Books:

Hathaway House
Aaron, Book 1
Brock, Book 2
Cole, Book 3
Denton, Book 4
Elliot, Book 5
Finn, Book 6
Gregory, Book 7
Heath, Book 8
Iain, Book 9
Jaden, Book 10
Keith, Book 11
Lance, Book 12
Melissa, Book 13
Nash, Book 14

The K9 Files
Ethan, Book 1
Pierce, Book 2
Zane, Book 3
Blaze, Book 4
Lucas, Book 5
Parker, Book 6
Carter, Book 7
Weston, Book 8

Greyson, Book 9
Rowan, Book 10
Caleb, Book 11

Lovely Lethal Gardens
Arsenic in the Azaleas, Book 1
Bones in the Begonias, Book 2
Corpse in the Carnations, Book 3
Daggers in the Dahlias, Book 4
Evidence in the Echinacea, Book 5
Footprints in the Ferns, Book 6
Gun in the Gardenias, Book 7
Handcuffs in the Heather, Book 8
Ice Pick in the Ivy, Book 9
Jewels in the Juniper, Book 10
Killer in the Kiwis, Book 11
Lovely Lethal Gardens, Books 1–2
Lovely Lethal Gardens, Books 3–4
Lovely Lethal Gardens, Books 5–6

Psychic Vision Series
Tuesday's Child
Hide 'n Go Seek
Maddy's Floor
Garden of Sorrow
Knock Knock...
Rare Find
Eyes to the Soul
Now You See Her
Shattered
Into the Abyss
Seeds of Malice
Eye of the Falcon

Itsy-Bitsy Spider
Unmasked
Deep Beneath
From the Ashes
Stroke of Death
Ice Maiden
Psychic Visions Books 1–3
Psychic Visions Books 4–6
Psychic Visions Books 7–9

By Death Series
Touched by Death
Haunted by Death
Chilled by Death
By Death Books 1–3

Broken Protocols – Romantic Comedy Series
Cat's Meow
Cat's Pajamas
Cat's Cradle
Cat's Claus
Broken Protocols 1-4

Broken and... Mending
Skin
Scars
Scales (of Justice)
Broken but… Mending 1-3

Glory
Genesis
Tori
Celeste

Glory Trilogy

Biker Blues
Morgan: Biker Blues, Volume 1
Cash: Biker Blues, Volume 2

SEALs of Honor
Mason: SEALs of Honor, Book 1
Hawk: SEALs of Honor, Book 2
Dane: SEALs of Honor, Book 3
Swede: SEALs of Honor, Book 4
Shadow: SEALs of Honor, Book 5
Cooper: SEALs of Honor, Book 6
Markus: SEALs of Honor, Book 7
Evan: SEALs of Honor, Book 8
Mason's Wish: SEALs of Honor, Book 9
Chase: SEALs of Honor, Book 10
Brett: SEALs of Honor, Book 11
Devlin: SEALs of Honor, Book 12
Easton: SEALs of Honor, Book 13
Ryder: SEALs of Honor, Book 14
Macklin: SEALs of Honor, Book 15
Corey: SEALs of Honor, Book 16
Warrick: SEALs of Honor, Book 17
Tanner: SEALs of Honor, Book 18
Jackson: SEALs of Honor, Book 19
Kanen: SEALs of Honor, Book 20
Nelson: SEALs of Honor, Book 21
Taylor: SEALs of Honor, Book 22
Colton: SEALs of Honor, Book 23
Troy: SEALs of Honor, Book 24
Axel: SEALs of Honor, Book 25
SEALs of Honor, Books 1–3

Heroes for Hire

Heroes for Hire, Books 1–3
Heroes for Hire, Books 4–6
Heroes for Hire, Books 7–9
Heroes for Hire, Books 10–12
Heroes for Hire, Books 13–15

SEALs of Steel
Badger: SEALs of Steel, Book 1
Erick: SEALs of Steel, Book 2
Cade: SEALs of Steel, Book 3
Talon: SEALs of Steel, Book 4
Laszlo: SEALs of Steel, Book 5
Geir: SEALs of Steel, Book 6
Jager: SEALs of Steel, Book 7
The Final Reveal: SEALs of Steel, Book 8
SEALs of Steel, Books 1–4
SEALs of Steel, Books 5–8
SEALs of Steel, Books 1–8

The Mavericks
Kerrick, Book 1
Griffin, Book 2
Jax, Book 3
Beau, Book 4
Asher, Book 5
Ryker, Book 6
Miles, Book 7
Nico, Book 8
Keane, Book 9
Lennox, Book 10
Gavin, Book 11
Shane, Book 12

Bullard's Battle Series
Ryland's Reach, Book 1
Cain's Cross, Book 2
Eton's Escape, Book 3
Garret's Gambit, Book 4
Kano's Keep, Book 5
Fallon's Flaw, Book 6
Quinn's Quest, Book 7
Bullard's Beauty, Book 8

Collections
Dare to Be You…
Dare to Love…
Dare to be Strong…
RomanceX3

Standalone Novellas
It's a Dog's Life
Riana's Revenge
Second Chances

Published Young Adult Books:

Family Blood Ties Series
Vampire in Denial
Vampire in Distress
Vampire in Design
Vampire in Deceit
Vampire in Defiance
Vampire in Conflict
Vampire in Chaos
Vampire in Crisis
Vampire in Control

Vampire in Charge

Family Blood Ties Set 1–3

Family Blood Ties Set 1–5

Family Blood Ties Set 4–6

Family Blood Ties Set 7–9

Sian's Solution, A Family Blood Ties Series Prequel
Novelette

Design series
Dangerous Designs

Deadly Designs

Darkest Designs

Design Series Trilogy

Standalone
In Cassie's Corner

Gem Stone (a Gemma Stone Mystery)

Time Thieves

Published Non-Fiction Books:

Career Essentials
Career Essentials: The Résumé

Career Essentials: The Cover Letter

Career Essentials: The Interview

Career Essentials: 3 in 1

Printed in Great Britain
by Amazon

15149990R00108